With A Wink
And A Nod

With A Wink And A Nod

Dallas A. Davis

Copyright © 2015 by Dallas A. Davis.

Library of Congress Control Number:		2015919769
ISBN:	Hardcover	978-1-5144-3009-5
	Softcover	978-1-5144-3008-8
	eBook	978-1-5144-3007-1

All rights reserved. No part of this book may be reproduced or transmitted in any form or by any means, electronic or mechanical, including photocopying, recording, or by any information storage and retrieval system, without permission in writing from the copyright owner.

This is a work of fiction. Names, characters, places and incidents either are the product of the author's imagination or are used fictitiously, and any resemblance to any actual persons, living or dead, events, or locales is entirely coincidental.

Any people depicted in stock imagery provided by Thinkstock are models, and such images are being used for illustrative purposes only. Certain stock imagery © Thinkstock.

Print information available on the last page.

Rev. date: 12/02/2015

To order additional copies of this book, contact:
Xlibris
1-888-795-4274
www.Xlibris.com
Orders@Xlibris.com
730475

Contents

Chapter I	Starting Over	1
Chapter II	The Meeting	9
Chapter III	Experiments	13
Chapter IV	The Caller	15
Chapter V	My New Condo	19
Chapter VI	Old Friends	22
Chapter VII	Planning Stage	31
Chapter VIII	Friends And Good Food	33
Chapter IX	Meeting Cora	37
Chapter X	The Compound	40
Chapter XI	Separate Flights	46
Chapter XII	Back To Reality	54
Chapter XIII	More Arrivals	57
Chapter XIV	The Rest Of The Team	62
Chapter XV	A Little R & R	64
Chapter XVI	Tense Moments	67
Chapter XVII	Bomb Scare	71
Chapter XVIII	Romance	73
Chapter XIX	I Do	75
Chapter XX	The Gab Session	77
Chapter XXI	The Preparation	93
Chapter XXII	One Last Cook-Off	98
Chapter XXIII	The Trip West	102
Chapter XXIV	Mending Fences	109
Chapter XXV	Reminiscing	111
Chapter XXVI	The Discovery	116
Chapter XXVII	Outlandish Acts	120
Chapter XXVIII	Unexpected Discovery	127
Chapter XXIX	Pondering Our Next Step	132
Chapter XXX	Saving Trudy	135
Chapter XXXI	Meeting The Children	138

Chapter XXXII   The Adoption Process 142
Chapter XXXIII The Finale 146

Author's Note 153
About the Author 155

Chapter I

STARTING OVER

As I snuggle into my husbands loving, comfy, yet strong arms I reflect on my life and become composed in my thoughts. I think back to the day my life was changed forever. . .

#

A tranquil rain is falling. Winter is being washed away, preparing the earth for a new season. It is rather warm for the 25th of March in New England.
"Did March come in like a lion or lamb? "Must have come in like a lion, because it is surely going out like a lamb." I don't usually talk to myself, but it has been a long and difficult winter. I chuckle to myself as my mother's euphemisms creep into my thoughts. She always said, "If there is a ring around the moon, it's going to rain the next day". Or, "If the new moon is tipped down, it is going to rain the next day. If it is tipped up, it will hold the rain in and it won't rain". I get such a kick out of her. These euphemisms have been handed down generation to generation for many centuries.
The landscape is extraordinary and I am absorbing it into my thoughts, trying to escape the disturbing past that has brought me to this time and place.
The buds on the trees are just starting to burst forth. Unyielding wild crocuses are pushing their proud spikes through the dead leaves left behind in the un-raked yards. A raw, green haze blankets the roadside. A whiff

of clean fresh air comes through the car window that is lowered about two inches, and brushes past my face.

I take a deep breath and *sigh*. "Ah spring", I whisper. It means new life. The windshield wipers are groaning they're usual tune, *urrrup, urrrip, urrrup, urrrip*.

I drive a Lincoln. I love my Lincoln because of its comfort and size. The mileage isn't the greatest, but comfort and performance are much more important to me. The massive trunk capacity is also a priority for me, as my few precious mementos must go with me whenever I move from place to place.

The sun finally peeks through the clouds and overtakes the gloom and everything glistens like diamond dust being sprinkled from the sky. Gradually appearing, as if a sign, a radiant double Rainbow ascends above the horizon.

This will be my turning point. . .my new beginning. I drive on, not really knowing my destination, when I approach a sign that reads, "Worcester-20 miles". <u>This must be the place. The name of the city sounds familiar, though I have never been in Worcester that I can recall. It just feels like it might be a nice place to settle down.</u>

My name is Dr. Laura Willows. People say I have a distinguished manner. When I enter a room I feel heads turning in my direction. My friends say I have the grace of a gazelle, because I am tall and slender and hold my head high, as if I haven't a care in the world. My dark brown hair, which I wear in a chignon, has a healthy shine to it. My eyes are golden hazel and appear to change color from brown to golden, depending on what I am wearing. I wear some makeup, but not a lot. I pride myself on my blemish free complexion that I inherited from my mother. I never went through the acne stage as a teenager. Although I have my mother's complexion, I favor my father in appearance and stature.

Recollections of the events that led to leaving my last position are emblazoned in my thoughts. I try not to think about it, but there is no way to erase such a tragedy. I keep having flashes of the past clamoring in my head as I approach the City of Worcester, Massachusetts. <u>"No! I cannot believe that I could have been that preoccupied, to have poisoned my colleagues,"</u> I yell out loud. The sound of my own voice startles my serenity. My life at the lab is being repeated over and over in my mind, as if lived by a stranger.

#

I was employed by the government at their experimental lab in Bethesda, Maryland. I was one of their top scientists, also one of the youngest. I never felt that the men who dominated the personnel at the lab expected more out of me because I was one of only three females. Quite the opposite...they seemed to have a great deal of respect for me. One day a few of us worked on a project that took us into the late evening hours. We developed a formula for a lethal solution; a formula that could very possibly eliminate mankind. The Russians had developed a similar solution and the United States government wanted to be sure they could duplicate it. In doing so, one would balance out the other and there would be no threat coming from Russia or any other country that might want to do harm to the United States. Before an antidote could be developed, somehow a few drops of the formula found its way into the bottle of drinking water in my department.

Neither my colleagues nor I would have laced the water on purpose, but it did happen. I searched my mind trying to think of how the formula could have gotten into the water. The only explanation I could muster was perhaps when a new bottle of water was placed into the dispenser, the person who replaced it must have had some of the lethal solution on his or her hands; and it got into the cooler. As a result, two of my colleagues died after drinking the water. Even though we always wore sterile gloves, sometimes, in our haste, we might forget to take our gloves off before taking on another task. Because I was in charge of that department, I took the full blame for the tragedy.

Why didn't anyone investigate the accident? I wondered. No investigation ever took place. . .only accusations. Everything was swept under the rug. . .my dismissal. . .closing the case. . .with a conclusion that death was due to negligence of the scientists. I was told, however, my records will show my culpability for the entire occurrence. I was devastated; the sheer horror of it all blocked everything else from my mind.

I could do nothing about it. After all, I would have been challenging the government, I thought. The disgrace is etched forever in my mind. I liked the people I worked with and those two scientists are a great loss to the science world. As I look back there was only one person whom I disliked...that was my immediate boss, Dr. Charles Knight. There was just something about him that made me uncomfortable and for some reason I distrusted him. Do you know how sometimes you get a vibe from someone that you just don't trust them? That's how I felt about Dr. Knight. I always got the creeps when he was around me.

#

As my thoughts start to fade I pull into the parking lot of a neighborhood pharmacy. As I enter the store I search for the local newspaper. I see that it is a quaint little pharmacy with a soda fountain and a few tables and chairs. I order a strawberry frappe, grab a paper and look for a place to sit. Searching the want ads I find there are only a few positions available for someone with my qualifications. I need a job that will consume my thoughts, so I won't think about the past. Settling down in a city where no one knows me is a priority.

I see there is an opening at an abortion clinic. Although it goes against my moral values, I don't want to quibble at a time like this; a time of desperation; a time of forgetting and a time for a new life. Though I am a respected doctor and scientist, I can't forget what brings me to this time and place.

There is also an ad for a position at a local hospital for an ER doctor. It is Wednesday and I decide on the abortion clinic, hoping for an interview before the week is out. The abortion clinic is preferred, because I can be a little more anonymous than if I went to work in a large hospital. I want to keep low-key because I am so tormented by the tragedy at the lab.

In need of a place to stay I look around the pharmacy to see if I can find a clerk, or someone, who looks like they are one of the locals to ask about a hotel or boarding house.

I finish my frappe and tuck the want ads under my arm. I don't want to end up in a bad neighborhood, so I ask the person at the checkout counter where the best hotel is. She is slight in build and has a surprisingly low voice. She gives me directions to the Bancroft Hotel, a grand old landmark, where I check into a lovely oversized room.

I am quite pleased with the city of Worcester so far. The down town area is very appealing to a stranger. The store fronts are clean and very well dressed. I was very content with the thought of a tranquil life after the meat grinding life I just left. There were days when I didn't even go home. I would sleep on a cot at the lab and begin my next day with a kink in my neck.

The Bancroft Hotel is an impressive structure, built in the 1920's, I am told. A beautiful, fifteen-story building made of granite and concrete, with floral scrolls surrounding the very top of the building. As I enter the main lobby, I see the now familiar old Baroque splendor with beautiful marble floors and expensive Persian rugs underlining the furniture. Overstuffed leather easy chairs and sofa, polished to a high sheen, welcomes the guests. As I approach the front desk, I touch solid walnut gleaming to a rich gloss, as are the walls around it. A neatly dressed concierge greats me and checks me into my room.

Across the street from the main entrance I observe The City Common; a beautiful park with war memorials, fountains, benches and crisscross cement walkways. At the west end of The Common is City Hall; a majestically domed concrete building that resembles the Capitol building in Washington, D. C.

My room overlooks The Common below. As I enter the room, I notice a small refrigerator under a bar in one corner. This is a must for me, as I like my midnight snacks. There is a writing desk in the opposite corner next to a queen-sized bed and a sofa and chair at the other end. The extra space is needed, because my stay will be prolonged while I look for a permanent place to live.

The closet space is small but ample enough to hold my limited wardrobe, as my working attire consists of a dark skirt, off white blouse, and a pink smock. My social life is very occasional; a few evening and jogging clothes are all that is needed. I love to wear nice clothes, but not having enough time to shop or date, I have a very limited wardrobe.

After settling in my room, I realize that it is definitely time for me to start over. I've had enough time to ponder what happened at the lab and to lick my wounds. "Laura," I say, as I look into the mirror, "You have come full circle, it is now time to forget about the past and begin a new chapter in your life." It's as though my mother is speaking these words to me.

Once I settle in my room, I dial the phone number of the clinic. I hear a melodic voice say, *"East Side Clinic, this is Trina, how may I help you?"*

"Hello, my name is Dr. Laura Willows, and I am answering your ad in the Worcester Telegram. It says you are in need of a physician at your clinic."

The person on the other end says, *"Hi, Dr. Willows. We certainly are in need of a physician."*

"Would it be possible to have an appointment sometime this week for an interview, Trina?"

"I can give you an appointment today, if you are available."

"Yes, I'm available. How soon would you like me to come in?"

"Great, can you be here in an hour?"

"I sure can," I answered, "but I will need directions, I just arrived in town."

I had on my robe, having freshly showered after driving all day. I quickly change into my street clothes, grab my briefcase that holds all my credentials and a copy of my résumé, and head out the door. "Oops, I almost left without my keys!"

From the Bancroft Hotel, it takes me only twenty minutes to drive to the clinic. The outside of the building, a concrete block painted light grey, looks ordinary and unremarkable. The Eastside Clinic is in a poorer part of town on Oxford Street near the railroad tracks.

As I walk through the front door, the openness and cleanliness of the interior strikes me. There is a couch and three plush chairs that dominate the attractively decorated waiting room. Magazines sit on shelves under each of the two end tables, which hold polished brass lamps.

I step to the receptionist's area and introduce myself to a young woman with the most beautiful brown skin. "Hi, I'm Dr. Laura Willows. You must be Trina."

"Oh, hi, I've been waiting for you. . .come with me." A bouncy little woman jumps to her feet. She stands only five feet tall, weighs about 98 pounds, and can't be more than 22 years old with the energy of a two year old.

I follow her down the hall past three examining rooms equipped with the usual exam tables and the dreaded stirrups. As I go by the first office, I pause briefly to notice the plush chairs and oak desk. Several nice prints of artwork hang on the walls. I recognize "The Café Terrace" by Van Gogh and "The Bridge at Argenteuil" by Monet. The second office is decorated similarly. *They certainly have made this place look inviting for the patients. This isn't at all what I had expected of an abortion clinic,* I think to myself. Trina ushers me into the room marked "Office Manager" and introduces me to Dr. Timothy Cramer before she leaves.

As he glances up from his papers, I see a pleasant looking man in his mid-fifties with graying hair, full beard and mustache. He immediately rises from his chair and extends his hand. He cups my hand with both of his in a friendly, firm handshake. *I like a firm handshake. It tells a lot about a person.*

As I sit down, I see that his office is agreeably decorated in comforting tones and warm colors. I think to myself, *someone around here has very good taste in decorating.*

As I hand him my résumé he adjusts his reading glasses and begins to read. The interview doesn't take very long. Dr. Cramer seems anxious to fill the position.

My credentials are impeccable: A graduate, with honors, from Johns Hopkins University, majoring in Biomedical Engineering and Baby Development, with an internship at Johns Hopkins University Medical Center. *I don't like to brag, but my GPA was 4.0. So I guess I do like to brag.*

Actually, the last four years of my work experience have been modified by the government, so that no one would know I worked on top secret projects in the research lab. But, luckily, neither would they be able to discover the little predicament that got me terminated.

After a few minutes Dr. Cramer looks up and says, "You have a very impressive résumé."

"Thank you, Doctor. I worked very hard for it."

A slight frown creases his brow. "Frankly, I am curious as to why you would want to work in an abortion clinic?"

The truth is, after the mess at the experimental lab, I am willing to take anything I can get in the line of employment. "Well," I say, thinking fast and trying to act confident and cool, "I like the working hours. I would like to spend more time pursuing some personal interests; and being on call at a hospital would interfere with my personal endeavors." I thought this reasoning might work out better for the time being.

He nods agreeably. "One of our doctors has retired and I am going on to other fields. Worcester is an old and very conservative city. There is a great shortage of doctors in Worcester who are willing to perform abortions."

I sense that what he really wants to say is: The clinic is desperate to hire another doctor willing to do abortions. If he only knew how un-willing I am.

He glances at my résumé once again. The wheels seem to be clicking in his head, but he finally looks up with a smile. "Well, Dr. Willows, the job is yours, if you want it."

"I should tell you, we are not funded by Planned Parenthood. We are here to help young girls by giving them an abortion so they can get on with their lives. I personally do not agree with Planned Parenthood and their philosophy or their politics. We are funded by charitable donations and the kindness of the citizens of Worcester." Dr. Kramer adds.

Feeling a great relief wash over me, I respond firmly. "That sounds fine with me. When would you like me to start?"

"How about Monday? We open at 9:00 a. m. and we close at 5:30 p. m. and we are closed on the weekends." We discuss salary and I agree with the amount.

"I think I can manage that." I stand up and extend my hand. He clasps my hand and says, "Welcome aboard Doctor."

"Thank you Dr. Cramer. See you Monday at nine."

I spend the next few days looking for a condo with no luck at all. Everything is either too large or too small. My room at the Bancroft can be rented by the month, which makes it a little more cost friendly, because my savings are not going to last forever.

Never having time for a social life, I have acquired an adequate savings account. Having moved frequently for my career, I have accumulated wealth from the profits on reselling my various homes. One of the many things my father taught me was that I should always buy; never rent. He would say, "All you are doing is filling someone else's pockets when you rent, and you never have anything to show for it." This and many other bits of useful information, is embedded into my memory from the wisdom of my beloved father.

Chapter II

THE MEETING

After filling out the usual papers for employment, my first two days at the clinic are spent acquainting myself with the staff and the workings of the clinic. Dr. Cramer commits to stay for two weeks until I get my bearings. Trina takes me around and introduces me to three nurses, two doctors and a secretary. They seem like very caring and decent people. There is one nurse in particular, Mary Jean Ashbury, to whom I take a liking right away.

As I look at Mary Jean, I see a very attractive woman. As we get to know each other over lunch on the second day she confides in me, "I'm in my 40's, married with three kids. I guess you could say I'm married in name only. My husband, Howard, took a hike after our third child was born. He told me he didn't like being tied down any more, and out the door he went with his suitcase in hand. Neither one of us has ever filed for divorce. I probably would have filed, but I have no idea where to find him.

I always had a suspicion that he ran off with the young secretary in his office. He was a used car salesman. She mysteriously disappeared around the same time Howard disappeared."

Mary Jean is medium height with short brown hair, and as she talks her beautiful green eyes are always smiling. Her skin has the glow of a freshly washed face and she wears a tinge of lipstick. I think to myself, *with a little makeup, Mary Jean would be a very stunning woman. She is very attractive, but we can all use a little help now and then.*

Mary Jean goes on to say, "I'm a registered nurse. I spent several years in Obstetrics at Brigham & Women's Hospital in Boston; one of the area's better hospitals. The only reason I came to the clinic is because they offered me a lot more money than I was making at the hospital. I'm not too keen on abortions; I'm pro-life. But after all, I have to feed and clothe those three kids, with no help from Howard. I only hope God will forgive me for working in an abortion clinic."

As I get to know Mary Jean I can see that she is a very strong and sensible woman, who realizes that she can never depend on anyone but herself. She has sacrificed her own dreams so she can make a nice life for her kids. She says, "I know they will never have a father to depend on, so I have to play both roles of father and mother. I try to be caring and loving when they need it and stern with my discipline when they need it." She proudly shows me pictures of her three children.

I comment, "They sure are good looking kids. They take after you I suspect?"

Mary Jean mentions she has never talked badly about their father in front of them. "When they ask about him, I tell them that he needed to get away and find himself. After all, he is still their father." She continues, "I see no need to turn the children against him. I always think that some day he might come back and want to see them, but I'm not holding my breath for that to happen."

#

Heading into my second month at the clinic, I enter the examining room where a new patient named Martha is waiting in her tight jeans and sweatshirt. Her brown hair, cut very short in a wispy style, frames her delicate face. From her chart, I can see that she has just turned 18, stands five-feet-three-inches tall, and weighs 105 pounds.

"Hello, Martha," I say in a friendly manner to ease the fright I see in her blue eyes. "Tell me about yourself."

"I got pregnant," she stammers glumly. "My boyfriend got cold feet and doesn't want the baby. I don't know what to do."

What is it with these boys who keep shrugging their responsibilities. Girls don't get pregnant all by themselves. And why can't girls have a little more respect for themselves. I set my chart down and put my hand on her arm to comfort her. I could feel her tremble. "We will see what we can do to help you. Did you get the packet of literature from the receptionist?"

She nods. A twinkle of hope in her big blue eyes makes her look like a little pixy. I believe she is still trying to talk herself into an abortion.

"Well, you know that the final decision is up to you. Did you read about the other options available to you? I can only imagine that it is a hard decision to face alone." Her head goes down as she lets out a deep sigh. She shakes her head from side to side.

"I don't know. . .I just don't know if I can do this." Tears form on the rims of her sad eyes.

"East Side Clinic is privately owned, and they do not discourage nor encourage abortions. It is completely left up to the patient. The patient is given brochures on the subject, pro and con, so they can make up their minds with full knowledge of what to expect either way. Although some abortion clinics do not do this, Worcester is a very conservative city; therefore the clinic deems it important to provide all the information they can to the women who seek help. It also provides information on giving up the child for adoption."

The phone rings just as Martha is starting to feel more at ease. I excuse myself and answer the phone. I recognize the voice on the other end immediately. I am puzzled as to why he is seeking me out, or even how he found me. *Surely my work with them is finished*. I ask Martha to go into the waiting room while I take the call. "Martha, would you please ask Trina to hold the rest of my calls?"

"Be glad to."

"Thanks, I won't be long,"

The voice on the other end says, "I want to meet with you at your earliest convenience." It is Dr. Charles Knight, the Lab Director in Bethesda, as he continues with his lecture he is very forceful and persistent that I not try to duck him or ignore him.

I tell him, "There is a little out-of-the way diner on June St., I could meet you there in about three hours."

He seems to be irritated and I get the feeling he wants to meet sooner, but then agrees to the arrangement. I told him, "That is the soonest I can get away, take it or leave it." I give him instructions on how to get to the diner and I hang up. *I wonder what that's all about?* I sure don't look forward to seeing him again.

I call Martha back into my office and after a lot of discussion we schedule her abortion for the next day. The young woman seems so unsure about the whole thing. I try to tell her that everything will turn out okay.

Just as I am walking Martha to the door she bursts into tears and I put my arms around her and give her a reassuring hug, saying, "It's normal to have these feelings. Why don't you consider talking to your parents? You will be surprised how parents can understand when we need them to."

"I'll think about it. My parents are great people and they have always supported me on everything in the past, but what are they going to think of me when they hear about this? My parents aren't rich, Dr. Willows.

My mother is a waitress and my father was just laid off from his job at the shoe factory."

"It doesn't matter how much money they have or don't have. I'm sure they would be willing to help you raise your child, if you choose to keep it."

Even though a doctor should be neutral, I sense that Martha comes from a good family and I feel she should at least give her parents a chance to know what is going on with her. Silently, I pray Martha will take my advice.

Chapter III

EXPERIMENTS

Some of the work I did at the lab, while working for the government was very covert. Biomedical experiments were performed in my particular lab. Not too many people knew about the things that went on in there. We were a hand picked group who were commissioned to study genetic engineering in humans. Some of the experiments were very technical. I had moral misgivings about some of the experiments, but I didn't question the government's motives.

My expertise was to duplicate specific genetic traits in multiple human embryos. What we did is a lot more complicated, but that's a simplified description.

The experiments were performed on aborted fetuses and mice. I was told that they made arrangements with an abortion clinic to furnish the specimens. I worked on the aborted fetuses that were preserved in formaldehyde.

I was very good and intensely thorough at what I did. Some of the experiments could only be performed on live specimens; this is where the live mice came into play. I realized that for most of my experiments, a live fetus would have been the qualifying model. I also realized that this would be too gruesome for my moral convictions. For the sake of science I did what I was told.

The project director told me that their experiments were going to help preserve mankind in case there is a catastrophic mishap on earth and Mankind would have to colonize on other planets. This made sense, because from all reports, NASA was looking for places, other than Earth, in which the atmosphere would be suitable for humans. If such a place existed, they would need to have ways of getting there and surviving. If a planet could be found in another galaxy, it would take many years to travel there, and they needed to know just how they would survive the trip and procreate.

Another phase of our research was to try to find cures or preventive medicines for debilitating diseases such as Multiple Sclerosis, Muscular Dystrophy, spinal injuries, Alzheimer's, Cancer, etc. Stem Cell research is essential for finding a cure for these diseases. There has been some concern in the public arena that Stem Cell research is no different from abortion or murder. As a scientist, I view this type of research much differently. The result of using Stem Cells in research far out-weighs any moral issue that may be entering into the equation. Most of the experiments are performed on a miscarried Embryo or an aborted Embryo. I developed a way of aborting the embryo and keeping it alive. I was very enthusiastic about that part of my research; even though I am pro-life, I only developed this for a scientific cause, not for the abortion motive.

I am still heartsick about the accident that killed my colleagues. Being a secretive project, there is a big cover-up. There was never any indication of any maliciousness. It was simply an error, a horrible error, which caused the death of two brilliant scientists. The memory of it will haunt my thoughts forever.

That phone call has brought back all the memories of that heartbreaking day at the lab. I have been trying to put all that behind me, and now my nightmare is returning. *<u>I really need to stop this pity party and get on with my life. What in the world can Charles possibly want with me now? Perhaps he is still thinking about using live fetuses for his experiments,</u>* I thought. *<u>After all I did develop a way to do just that. I just never thought I would have to actually do it myself. Dear God, what is he up to?</u>*

Chapter IV

THE CALLER

I meet with Charles around 6:00 p.m. Our meeting takes place in a dingy little bar and cafe, so smoke filled I can hardly make out the faces of the patrons; which is good because they won't be able to see me either. I make out Charles' eyeglasses glistening in the flashing light from the juke box. He has found a table in the far corner of the cheap, dimly lit cafe. He has already ordered a coffee and two glasses of water. I order an iced tea from the waitress at the counter and proceed to the table to face Charles. I wished, later, that I had ordered a double shot of something.

There he is, the narcissistic **Dr. Charles Knight**. He is a small man with beady little eyes peering through wire-framed glasses, with his usual bow tie fastened to his collar. A fashion plate, he is not. He is the Senior Director at the Federal Lab Facility. He was the one responsible for my dismissal. He has a stern, yet oddly devious, look on his face. We were never close but we worked together on several projects. I did hold a certain respect for him. He is a brilliant man and knows how to use his intelligence to his advantage. I did not extend my hand to him; although he made a move like he wanted to shake mine. I sat down feeling very uneasy.

"Laura, I have a proposal for you that I would urge you **not** to turn down. Keep in mind, that I have kept your personnel file."

In other words, he is letting me know, without actually saying it, that I am being blackmailed into going along with whatever scheme he has up his sleeve.

My back stiffened and I squared my shoulders and stated, "I'm willing to listen to what you have to say, but the final decision will be mine. This is, after all, still a free country. I don't know what you want, but I don't work for you any more and I would like to get on with my life and forget about the events that took place at the lab."

He takes me completely by surprise when he says, "No, you won't have to make a decision, Dr. Willows, it has already been made for you. Keep in mind, the accident that killed two of your colleagues."

"Oh, I see," I whisper, as I slump into my seat. I can feel the blood drain from my face and I start to feel a little queasy. An utterly eerie feeling comes over me and I feel as if I am going to faint. I never did trust Charles that much. Highly intelligent people scare me for some reason, especially those who have no close friends. If I didn't have to work with him, I would never have given him the right time of day. I am horrified at the thought of being threatened by this narcissistic gnome. He apparently notices the blood rush from my face and offers me a sip of water. I wave the offer off with a flick of my hand.

"Laura, do you remember the project, on which you worked?"

"Yes, indeed, I remember. I had developed a way to perform an abortion by keeping the fetus alive. What about it?"

"After you left the facility, the Project continued to progress with great enthusiasm; however, we have taken the project to new heights. We need your help with the next phase of our work."

"How can I help? I'm no longer affiliated with the Project. You made sure of that."

He proceeds to explain as much of the new project as he is willing to discuss with me at this time. I get the gist of the big picture quite rapidly. Now I see just how I fit into his little plan.

"You see Laura; we now need live fetuses for our project. We will expect you to furnish those for us."

I am the perfect "patsy" for their little project, as I am in the right place at the right time. Right for them that is; not so right for me. Why in the world did I take that position at the abortion clinic, I think to myself. *I'm completely against abortions. I should have had better judgment.*

"What about all the other Abortion facilities around the country that we used to use? You already have an account with them. Why don't you go to them with this project?"

His answer was vague, but I knew I should have established that, of course, he is in the process of contacting or has already contacted quite a few of the other Clinics. I am sure he must have his little "Patsies" everywhere. Now I am really beginning to doubt whether I am responsible for the mistake that killed those people. *Was it indeed, a set up?* He seems to be intensely sure of himself that he will have no trouble convincing others around the country to go along with this wicked scheme. I am trying to imagine who else might be in on all this from the Center. I can't really think of anyone except maybe a couple of people who would be working with him on this project. I'm thinking perhaps he has people outside of the Center who are working with him. I wonder. . .

Charles explains further just how I will go about handling most of the particulars. "I have people already in place to do what needs to be done. You are not to worry about any of the details just yet. All you have to do is be sure the aborted fetuses are handled properly."

"How am I supposed to do this without the people, with whom I work, wondering what I'm doing?"

"We will be placing some of our own people at your facility, so you shouldn't have trouble in that department. You will follow a format and everything will look sterile. We will be in touch with all the details for you to proceed on a need-to-know basis. We would like to get this program initiated as soon as possible. We have the proper accommodations in place and are waiting for our first shipments."

"How long have you worked on this, Charles? When I left the Center, you were working on something quite different."

"Not really. The government had this project in mind for years, and we just needed you and the others to work out some of the details."

"Are you telling me that I worked on this project and didn't even know what I was working on?"

"That is correct." He then starts to get up from his chair and hesitates, saying, "We will have someone contact you in about a week. You will receive your complete instructions then, please follow them."

"Wait a minute, if you don't mind my asking, just how in the hell did you know where I was working?"

A smirk crosses his face. "That's easy...you're Social Security number. By the way, it was very accommodating of you to find a position with an abortion clinic. I couldn't believe my luck. I hadn't even given you a thought for this project until I found out you were working at an abortion clinic." He says with a nasty sneer as he saunters out of the bar.

"And I thought I was choosing the abortion clinic so I would be less conspicuous. I guess I didn't count on this."

I sit there for about ten minutes to collect myself. Images are spinning in my head. Images of when Charles and I worked on a certain project together. I am desperately trying to remember if there is a hint or signal from him that any of this was going on. Nothing came to mind except one incident that occurred just before the "accident".

Charles mentioned something about using live fetuses and I jumped down his throat and call him "Frankenstein", jokingly, of course. It dawns on me that he was probably feeling me out to see if I would go along with him or not. Now it all starts to make sense. I am aghast at the thought of using a live fetus, so maybe I'm not so far off when I think I'm being set up. Just two days after calling Charles a 'Frankenstein', the "accident" occurred. Those two scientists were very mindful and very intelligent people. They too were appalled at the thought of using live fetuses for experiments. My head is buzzing with unanswered questions. *"Too bad I gave up smoking right after college," I say to myself; "I would love a cigarette right about now."*

No matter how I look at it, I am being used big time and I am not happy about it. So, it looks like I'm locked into this project whether I want in or not; at least until I have proof that I was set up. Now, I have to try to convince the others at the clinic that I am legitimate. I never told anyone about the government project. I was sworn to secrecy when I left. They invented false credentials for my employment for the past four years. I had to go along with that, because of the secrecy in the work that I did along with the others at the Center.

I am mentally drained as I return to the Bancroft that night. I barely remember driving back to the Bancroft. I park my car in the lot and slowly walk through the front door of the building. My head is spinning and it isn't from alcohol. What Charles expects of me is an earth-shattering request, to say the least. I know what I have to do because when you work for the government, they own you for the rest of your life. *It is comparable to working for the FBI or the CIA, I thought, once an Agent, always an Agent. Only death can get you out of the government's clutches.* I'm not quite ready for that just yet. I have a lot more living to do. Now I'm thinking, this really doesn't sound like the government's work. I wonder if Charles is legit. As I enter my room I say to myself, *Oh, Laura, what have you gotten yourself into now?* I look at myself in the mirror and whisper, "Frankenstein!" I am completely repulsed by all of this. I wished I had never developed that method of keeping the fetus alive. I am more and more convinced that the government is not aware of Charles' intentions, whatever they may be. I can't imagine the Government being in on a project like this.

Chapter V

MY NEW CONDO

It is 3:00 a.m. before I finally fall asleep. I awake at 8:30 in the morning. I can barely open my eyes, "Holy cow, I'm going to be late for work." I stagger to my feet as the previous evening is still swirling in my head.

After some thought about whether to go to the clinic or not I resolve I need to take some time off to look for a permanent place to live.

I call the clinic and tell them to reschedule my morning appointments; I will be in after lunch. Just as I hang up the phone, it rings and it is my real estate Agent, Edgar.

He tells me, "I have a hot lead on a Condominium. I will get back to you in about a half hour. I just wanted to make sure you were there. I have a few things I need to check on first. Okay with you?"

"Absolutely!! You must be psychic, Edgar, I was just going to call you. I'll be waiting for your call." Excited about the prospects of a condo, I head for the bathroom and take a quick shower, get dressed and wait for Edgar to call me back.

Edgar Fleming is probably in his early to mid 60's. He looks a little like Col. Sanders, the famous chicken man, with his short gray beard and round smiling face. I met him while having lunch at one of the local diners. We struck up a conversation and he handed me his card. I told him I was interested in buying a condo. He says, "I have been in real estate all my adult life, at least 40 years. I know every house and piece of real estate in the entire City of Worcester. I know who lives where, who bought what and how much they paid for it. You could say I also know where the bodies are buried."

I am so glad Edgar called, "I must have sent him a mental message that I would be available today."

Edgar calls back exactly one half hour later and asks me to meet him in the lobby in 10 minutes. I am so excited I grab my coat and run for the elevator. I get to the lobby about seven minutes before Edgar arrives. He has a big smile on his face and says, "Follow me. We are going to walk to your new condo."

"Lead the way, Edgar, I can hardly wait," I motion for him to go out of the door first.

We walk across the Common to the building on the corner. I am bubbling with anticipation. He has an absolutely perfect condominium that I grab at first sight. The cost is a little more than I wanted to pay, but it is worth it. It is in a High Rise; however, this unit is on the second floor. This is perfect for me because I am not too thrilled about living in the clouds. I have a slight problem with heights. Edgar shows me the most perfect two bedroom, two-bath condo that I have ever seen. All the colors are exactly what I would have put in here. It has just been redecorated and the owners are looking for a quick sale. The kitchen is perfect, as I love to cook when I have time. Cooking is like therapy for me. I really get into it big time. A bay window in the Living room over-looks the Town Common. "Great View"! I tell him.

I am quite pleased about the fact that the building is across from the Common, as I like living in that area. They tore down the old Woolworth building, along with a few others, and built a condominium and a shopping Mall that encompasses the rest of the block.

After I move into my Condo, I will be able to continue my morning ritual. Every morning, about 5:30, I get into my jogging clothes and go for a slow jog for a mile around the perimeter of the Common. I was worried about moving elsewhere and not having the use of the Common. While I am jogging I reflect on the previous day's experiences and the coming day's events. I cherish my jogging time. It is my way of meditation. Some people meditate in a quiet room, or on the bus going to work, or just out for a stroll. I do my best thinking while jogging. It keeps me mentally and physically in shape.

#

As it turns out, they don't need me at the clinic that morning after all, because Martha decides to keep her baby. I am so pleased with this news. Martha had a long talk with her parents and they said they would help her with the baby if she decides to keep it, so long as she forgets about the no-show, weak-kneed boyfriend. This is no problem for her; she wants no part of him at all. So far as she is concerned, he doesn't exist. He is the one who wants her to have the abortion in the first place and then he just drops her at the clinic and takes off. *Nice guy.*

Martha comes to the clinic the next day to explain the decision she has made. She asks me, "Will you be my doctor through my pregnancy and delivery?"

I am flattered and happy for her, "I will be delighted to see you through your pregnancy and help with the delivery of your baby." It pleases me that Martha took my advice and talked to her parents. I prescribe some vitamins for her and instruct her on how to take care of her health and the baby's welfare.

Friday comes quickly that week and I am very satisfied with myself. I found a place to live, and, through my advice, a young 18-year-old woman is going to become a mother and keep her baby after all. I know Martha has a rough road ahead of her, but with her parents help, she will make it. In case you have forgotten, I am Pro-Life.

#

"Hey, it's a job," I tell my mother. When ever I feel that the walls are closing in on me I call my mother and use her as a sounding board. She always knocks those walls down for me.

I never talked to her about what happened at the other place, I hinted at something amiss, but she never questioned me about it.

She knows that when the time is right, she will be informed about everything.

Chapter VI

OLD FRIENDS

    I spend the weekend shopping for furniture. I enter Callahan's Furniture Store, which is just a few blocks from the Hotel. They have a great selection. It's not like most furniture stores; where everything seems the same old stuff you find everywhere. I find exactly what I want. I furnish my entire condo in one afternoon. I'm not much of a shopper so when I see something I like, I buy it. I don't do comparison-shopping. I don't have the time for that. I especially want to find a glass front hutch where I can display my blue Antique set that I found at a quaint Antique shop in Virginia. I find a beautiful dinning room set that has the perfect hutch. Everything is being delivered the following week, when I will be moving in. I finish my shopping at Shearer's Department Store and equip my kitchen and bathrooms. I don't like to waste a lot of time shopping. Some people like to go from store to store comparing prices. Not I...I want to get in and get out. Any miscellaneous items that I may need I can always get later; but the bulk of my shopping is done in two stores.

    I am a conservative person and whenever I move from one City or State to another, I sell most of my furnishings. I keep a few mementos but the rest can all be replaced when I reach my new destination. That way I'm not burdened with so much baggage; except the mental baggage that haunts me still.

#

Monday morning comes quickly, and not knowing what will be in store for me when *THEY* decided to contact me; I am a bit on edge. I don't have long to wait. They call me at nine o'clock in the morning and tell me my 'contact' will get in touch with me in a few days and that I am to follow his instructions to the letter. Well, at least I now know that my contact will be a man. I hope it isn't going to be Charles. I couldn't take much more of him.

The phone call comes the following Wednesday afternoon. To my pleasant surprise, it is one of my old cohorts, **Dr. Chauncey Sinclair**. We always got along great and I thought he was a terrific person. He was just about as upset as I when I left the lab in disgrace. Chauncey is a tall, gangly type with horn-rimmed glasses. With a slight twinkle in his eye. He has a great personality and sense of humor to match. He and I were always joking around. We became very close friends in the four years we worked together. He was married to what looked like his twin sister. I often wondered why they couldn't make the marriage work; they looked so suited to each other. Alma was tall and thin. She had no shape at all; but what a brilliant mind. They were in the process of a divorce when I left the facility. I heard that Alma left the project shortly after their divorce was final. I had a little crush on him but I never acted on it.

I recall Chauncey to be in his mid 40's, over six feet tall, weighing about 215 pounds; dark brown hair with a little gray at the temples. He has steel blue eyes that send tingles up my spine whenever he looks at me a certain way. He is clean-shaven, which is how I like a man to be.

Chauncey says, "I will be in Worcester the following Monday." We make arrangements to meet at a coffee shop down the street from the clinic. Chauncey said he didn't want to come to the clinic for obvious reasons. I say, "Call me when you get to town and we will set a time to meet."

That weekend I have my furniture delivered and I start arranging my Condo. I am thrilled with my new home. The furniture store sent two men to deliver the furniture and they help me place the items where I want them. They set up the beds in my bedroom and in the guest bedroom.

I immediately find my Antique glassware set, unwrap it and place it in the Hutch. I stand back to admire it and am very satisfied with my purchases.

#

As I look at my antique glassware I start to reflect on the last few months before I came to Worcester; a time when I tried not to think about my troubles. After leaving my last position, I decided to take a few months off to just motor around New England before looking for another place of employment. I stayed in the South Eastern Coast States at first; because of the winter weather in New England being so unpredictable, it was a safe bet to stay in the warmer areas until winter decides to make its exit.

I drive into Washington D. C. . .too early for the cherry blossoms. I have always been in love with Washington D.C. The Capitol building is breathtaking. I appreciate the monuments and the atmosphere of the City itself. It makes me feel like I'm in the company of greatness when I visit Washington, D.C.

After about two weeks in D. C., visiting museums and the art centers, I continue on my journey and drive into Virginia and find a quaint little Antique Shop in the small town of Midland. I spent about three hours in the shop. I spot an old piece of Hobnail Glassware. It reminds me of something my grandmother had in her home. As I look further, I find a condiment set of blue pressed diamond pattern, vinegar cruet, spoon holder, and creamer and covered sugar bowl. I read somewhere that the blue is very rare. *This, I cannot resist,* I say to myself.

As I walk through the shop I encounter the owner; a woman in her mid 60's, I thought. This tall, stately woman, with beautiful gray hair, stands at the counter. She carries herself with such grace. I sensed that she was quite stunning when she was younger. Actually, she is still rather attractive. She is wearing a gorgeous black Tunic sweater, with an embroidered green and rose colored floral pattern that flows down one side from the shoulder. I interrupt the silence of the shop and say, "Excuse me, would you mind if I ask you where you purchased your sweater? It's exquisite."

The woman smiled proudly and said, "Thank you, I knit it myself."

"Oh my, it's so elegant. You have a great talent."

"Well thank you again."

I paid for my purchase and started to leave. The women called after me, "Please, come have a cup of coffee and a piece of cake with me. You look like you could use a break and I know I could."

I turned and shook her hand and said, "I'd love to. Thanks for asking. I could use a cup of coffee. My name is Laura Willows." She ushers me into a cozy little room in the back of the store.

"I'm Carla Lightner; it is nice to meet you, Laura. Come, sit down here." She motions to a pressed-back chair with a lovely hand crocheted cushion. I enter the back room that is decorated like an old fashioned sitting room. As I look around I see a fainting couch against one wall; a handsome Victorian end table with an ornate silver Tea service displayed on it that sits next to a tapestry sofa. There is a Tiffany lamp on another table, which looks to be very old.

We sit at a small round table where teacakes are already on a plate. It is almost like Carla was waiting for someone with whom she could share her afternoon coffee and cake. We drink from cups, which Carla explains is part of her collection of Antique cups and saucers. <u>This is a very elegantly decorated room</u>, I thought. As I sit and chat with Carla and listen to some of her experiences. I reflect about my troubles at the government Lab and I realize how nice it is to sit and chat with a stranger, who knows nothing about me. How nice it is to sit and forget about my troubles, if only for a moment.

We chat for almost the entire afternoon. Carla says, "The shop isn't busy in the middle of the week. I usually do the bulk of my business on the weekends, so I enjoy a coffee break with a customer now and then."

Carla says, "I am from one of Midland's oldest family's; I'm a true native of Virginia. Most of the items in my shop are from my own family. I also take a few consignments from some of the locals."

"I was about to say that I have never seen so many elegant items in one store. I am very impressed with all the different and rare things you have here."

We enjoyed a nice chat but it was time for me to leave. <u>What a nice lady</u>, I thought as I left the shop with my great find. I took Carla's business card and said I would contact her when I get settled. I was interested in purchasing some other items that I saw in Carla's shop that really intrigued me. I normally don't look for Antique Shops, but something told me to go into this one. I'm not an antique collector but there are certain things that I like and want to display in my home. My mother and grandmother collected antiques, so I have been around them all my life.

From Midland, I drive on to Portsmouth, to visit, Ashley, my cousin. Whenever my parents went to Europe in the summer on military business, my sisters and brother and I stayed with our mother's sister, Katherine, who had three children of her own. They lived in a huge house, so there was always plenty of room for all of us. Katelyn, Ashley and Marc Jeffers are our cousin's. I visited with Ashley, who is my age. Ashley is married to Kevin Delaney and they have two children, Eric and Becky. Kevin works at Merrill Lynch in Portsmouth. Ashley and her family reside in the old family home. Katelyn and Marc live in another area of Portsmouth. Our cousin's parents were both killed in an auto accident while they were on vacation at Cape Cod, when Ashley was in college. They didn't want to sell the house so they turned it over to Ashley. It's a beautiful home and Ashley has a great eye for decorating.

I was planning to stay about three days, but they insisted that I stay longer. I ended up staying a little over three weeks. I really had a wonderful visit, since I always got along great with my cousins. We did a lot of reminiscing and we made tentative plans for another get-together very soon. Ashley gathered her siblings and their families for a dinner party one Sunday afternoon, so I could visit with everyone. Their children were absolutely a delight to talk to. They didn't seem to mind that I was of the 'older group'. I enjoyed my visit with Katelyn and Marc, whom I hadn't seen in many years. Ashley hated to see me leave and I hated to go. I could tell she knew something was bothering me, but I didn't bring up my troubles in conversation and Ashley didn't pry. I didn't want to put a damper on our visit. I was having enough trouble trying to figure it all out for myself. I didn't need to burden her with my troubles at this point. I will come around some day and tell her why I was troubled. There were a couple of moments when I could see that she wanted to ask me what was bothering me, but she held her tongue. The two of us were as close as two people can be. There were many times when we would finish each other's sentences.

I take Highway 17 out of Portsmouth and travel on up the coast. As I drive along, I remember the great times we always had with our cousins and aunt and uncle when we were young. I sometimes wish I could go back to those fun-loving and innocent days of my youth. It would be nice if we could just snap our fingers and all the bad stuff in our lives would go away.

I went through Washington D. C. again; and this time the cherry trees were in full bloom. What a wonderful sight. I then drove on through Allentown, Newark, and ended up in Hartford, Connecticut. I found a very nice Hotel in Hartford where I spent several days just shopping and looking up a few old friends I knew from college. I took Highway 84 on up to Highway 90 and then 290 into Worcester. I am so glad I stopped to visit with my cousins, as they kept me so busy I didn't have a chance to feel sorry for myself. It was a blessed visit.

#

Chauncey calls at noon on Monday. We set a time to meet at a coffee shop near the clinic. I give him directions and we meet there at one thirty p.m.

You could have knocked me over with a feather when I meet Chauncey for coffee. *<u>Oh boy, has he changed,</u>* I think to myself. *<u>No more horn rimmed glasses...contacts. He even put on a little weight and it looks like he's been working out at a gym.</u>* I almost didn't recognize him. In fact, I didn't. He spots me first and gives me a wave as I walk into the coffee shop. I almost trip over my tongue when I say, "I'm impressed, Chauncey, what have you done to yourself, you look fantastic." I give him a hug and a pick on the cheek.

He replies, "Nothing much, just some good cooking and a great trainer at the gym. "I took a few culinary lessons after Alma and I divorced, and I've became quite the chef. I never knew how much fun it is in the kitchen until I actually started cooking for myself."

I always called Chauncey, Chance, because he would never take a 'chance' on anything, whether it was an experiment or a lottery ticket. I used to chant at him, *"Chance, Chance, Scaredy-pants, afraid to take a Lottery Chance."* He has changed all right, and I like what I see.

We catch up on what each has been doing since our days at the Facility. He tells me he will be my only contact, and starts to tell about what my role will be in all of this.

I stop him short and suggest we meet at my place to carry on the rest of our conversation, as I don't care to discuss any of this in public. He agrees to meet at my condo after work. I explain to him that I just moved in and things are still in disarray. I give him another hug and tell him I have a few things to clear up at the clinic and then I will be home. I give him directions and I go back to the clinic.

Wow, those old feelings came back when I see him. I sure do have a thing for him. <u>I wonder if he has a thing for me.</u> I whisper to myself. <u>Okay, I say to myself, that's enough of that.</u>

It is almost closing time but I have to go back to the clinic to check up on a few things. I give Chance my address and instructions how to get there. And he is waiting for me on a Park Bench, in the Common, when I get home.

After fumbling for my key, we enter my condo, "I'm so sorry, how stupid of me, I should have given you my key so you didn't have to wait outside. You must be thirsty." I pour him a cold glass of water from the fridge.

He lets out a big sigh after he takes a well deserved quenching drink, and says, "Thanks, I guess I was more dehydrated than I realized. "But it's no big deal; I had some reading that I wanted to catch up on; and that beautiful park is very convenient for doing just that."

"Go and make yourself comfy and I will put the tea kettle on." I change into my 'comfy' clothes; and while we sip our wonderful herbal tea and nibble on the Danish I picked up on the way home; Chance fills me in on the details of our mission.

I'm thinking how handsome he looks in his dark blue suit. It is a great color on him. He is wearing a sky blue dress shirt and a pink and blue striped tie. I ask him, "Would you like to take off your jacket and loosen your tie?"

"I thought you would never ask. It sure is nice to be able to relax in comfort." I can see his powerful muscles as he stretches to take his jacket off. _Wow, he looks good._ He pauses for a moment and says, "This is the best herbal tea I have ever tasted. Where did you get it?"

"It's a special blend that I have made up for me. It is a combination of chamomile, hawthorn berries, orange peel, rose hips, crushed cherries and green tea. It is very relaxing. And it's also great over ice."

"I will have to get some of that for myself. It sure is delicious."

When he finishes telling me what my roll will be in this mission I stand and start to pace around the room and I tell him, "I have a tremendous reluctance about this whole thing. I find it rather malicious and I shudder to think of what you and Charles are involved in." I pause a moment and continue, "I thought Charles had one hell of a nerve expecting me to go along with his plans. . .no questions asked. If I have to go along with this debacle, I will, but I will be doing it under duress." I am so upset at this point tears are streaking down my face.

Chance takes a deep breath, jumps from his chair, "Thank God Almighty, you feel that way, Laura. Will you help me burn their Asses?" He says with a confrontational look on his face.

I throw my arms around his neck and, "Yes, Yes, Yes!" "Just tell me where to go, what to do, and how to do it."

At this moment we look into each other's eyes and Chance kisses me. At first his kiss is very soft, and when I react favorably toward the kiss, he seems to feel more confident and we melt into each other's arms. My body is dancing with joy. A tingle goes up and down my spine. I have never experienced this feeling before. What is happening to my body? I feel like a schoolgirl.

He pulls away quickly and says, "Gosh, I'm sorry, Laura, I guess I was caught up in the moment."

"No need to apologize, Chance, it was rather nice."

With a discomfited look on his face, he says, "I have wanted to do that since the first time I saw you."

"And I thank you for waiting, seeing as you were married the first time I saw you."

"I'm sorry if that kiss was unwanted."

"Oh no, just the contrary, you are quite welcome to that kiss." I assure him that I liked it just as much as he did. "I suppose I should confess that I have had a crush on you for a long time."

Chance has a startled look on his face and he says, "And I have had a crush on you ever since the first day we met." He kisses me again.

"Wow, I think we should concentrate on the problem at hand. I think I'm going to like being duplicitous. How about you?" My body was tingled all over and I thought I was going to faint from that kiss.

"Sorry, you're right. We need to make new plans."

Our conversation takes a sharp turn in another direction and we start to plot a new strategy. We aren't quite sure what our next step will be, but we know we have to act like we are on Charles' side of the fence and follow through with his orders.

Chance asks, "Do you think you can take Charles' orders without giving our position away?"

"You bet I can. I wasn't the lead in all those college plays for nothing."

(I find out very quickly that Chance is very altruistic. He never thinks of himself first. He would rather die than put another person at risk. In the weeks and months that follow, Chance has to bite the bullet and allow others to perform to their abilities.)

#

I'm still thinking of that kiss and silently hoping it means as much to him as it does to me. At this point I'm not too sure just what his motives are, so I try to play it cool, as if I couldn't care less whether we have a relationship or not. I try, however, not to be too nonchalant. I don't want to turn him off completely. Even though I had a little crush on him when we worked together at the Federal Lab; I never acted on it, because I'm just not the type to get involved with a married man. But it's open season now. Chance is about 11 years older than I and he and Alma appeared as though they were happy together.

I've never had a real relationship other than this one guy I almost married in college. I'm glad I came to my senses before I got hooked up with that loser. I heard a few years after graduating that he was bumming around Europe on his mommy and daddy's money.

I've had several male friends, but never had time for a serious relationship. Mainly, I was just looking for male companionship. When it comes to relationships with the opposite sex, I'm not too good at knowing what to do or how to feel. I'm feeling very different things going on in my body and my head that I have never felt before.

I am a 'tell it like it is' type person. I don't like to beat around the bush about anything. If I like someone, I tell him or her that I like him or her; if I don't like someone, I tell him or her to bug off.

When it comes to Chance, however, I am completely baffled about how to act around him. One minute I will be very confident and the next minute I will be a babbling idiot. There is some hope that Chance doesn't think I'm a complete idiot. I think, maybe that's what love is. It turns you into a babbling idiot.

#

After college, I went on to Medical school, then interned at Johns Hopkins Medical Center. From there I went right into the government job, so there wasn't a lot of time for men in my life.

I have always missed that bond with the opposite sex. I never gave it much thought until now. Being in Chance's arms just seemed so natural and right. For a split second, I think of us together as a couple, but then I quickly erase that thought from my mind. I am sure Chance thinks of me as just a colleague. Yet he did say he has wanted to kiss me from the first time he saw me. I think to myself. I will have to think about that a little longer.

#

Little do I know just how close Chance and I will become. We put our brains together and come up with a terrific scheme to bring this government project to its knees. "The bastards are not going to get away with this hideous program they have developed, in the name of 'Science'." I exclaim.

Chance is willing to finally take a risk, with me as his partner; and I am proud to be at his side. I have doubts at first, as we are going into uncharted waters with our eyes wide open, but not really knowing what to expect. Chance's knowledge of the set-up is a little vague, but he knows more than I. What he tells me is enough to make me want to vomit. Chance says, "We will have to go along with every detail of their plan so we don't throw suspicion on what we are really doing. I'm not sure just what Charles is up to, but I can assure you it isn't very kosher. I also think our government does not know what he is up to, otherwise they would have a little more information than they gave me."

I agree with what Chance is saying and add, "I plan to put on the greatest performance of my life. I have been wondering if this is all Charles' idea also. It seems a little too diabolic for our government to be involved."

Chapter VII

PLANNING STAGE

Chance doesn't have time to look for a place to stay, so I tell him about the Bancroft Hotel. He ponders it for a while and thinks he would be more comfortable in an apartment for the time being. I call Edgar and ask him if he lists any rentals. He said, "Yes I do, Laura, and I actually have a condo near your building that is for rent."

We make arrangements to go see the condominium the next evening and Chance likes it. It is more to his liking because of the privacy he will have there as opposed to a Hotel. Edgar told him he would have to clean and paint the place before Chance can move in, which is fine because he needs to buy furniture and equip the kitchen. I suggest my guest bedroom as a temporary accommodation until he can get settled into his own place. He takes me up on the offer.

The next day Chance goes shopping for his furniture. I direct him to Callahan's Furniture Store. He mentions that he is a friend of Dr. Laura Willows, and the salesman gives him a great deal on everything. It will all be delivered to his condo the following week. The most important piece of furniture for Chance is the lazy boy, with a built-in massager. Chance has a laid-back type personality but there is a lot of tension and stress in the work he does, so the lazy boy receives a good workout. Chance also joins the YMCA so he can stay in shape. I invite Chance to join me on my morning jogs, since we both enjoy exercise. I join Chance at the YMCA and we lift weights together. Chance says we will need to build our strength for the task ahead of us.

The next morning I contemplate my new role as an emissary and I am somewhat apprehensive about following orders and seeing that the aborted fetuses are handled properly. However, I know that the only way the plan will work is to follow every detail no matter how immoral the assignment may appear to me. An assistant is to be hired; one the Center will provide. A hefty donation comes to the clinic, anonymously. With this donation come instructions that I will be in charge of the entire Clinic and all its workings. I replace Dr. Cramer's position as supervisor, and the person, who is sent by Charles, will take over as my assistant and staff manager.

Mary Jean, for some reason, is able to keep her job, which makes me very happy. On the other hand, it makes me a little curious about Mary Jean, but I reconsider saying anything to her. If she is on Charles' payroll, it is not obvious to me. I ask Chance if Mary Jean is a "plant" and he says, "I don't think so, but I will check into it for you anyway." Trina is obviously no risk to anyone, so she stays on as the receptionist.

Chance asks, "Wasn't Mary Jean already at the clinic when you were hired?"

I said, "Oh, yes she was. I suppose I sound silly, but I would feel better if you check her out."

Chance knows just about every face that came and went at the Lab over the past six years. Chance never comes to the clinic. I arrange for him to see Mary Jean on our lunch break. We go to this great diner around the corner from the clinic. They serve that great "Truck Stop" food; the kind that we call comfort food. They serve that great stick-to-your-ribs kind of food that gets you through the rest of the day. Chance gets a good look at Mary Jean. He sits at the counter and orders a cup of coffee. He studies her face for quite a while and then makes his exit. He tells me later, "When I saw Mary Jean, I didn't recognize her face. Anyway, I think she looks too innocent to be on Charles' payroll."

She is such a good person. I am relieved that she is not with the project. Women need female companionship as well as male companionship. There are things we can talk about to another woman that we just aren't comfortable talking about with a man. Mary Jean's friendship means a lot to me. I hope my friendship also means a lot to Mary Jean.

Chapter VIII

FRIENDS AND GOOD FOOD

Mary Jean and I enjoy eating out once in a while. Her kids call me, Aunt Laura. She has me over to her house for dinner occasionally and sometimes to reciprocate, I will cook or take them all to Putnam & Thurston's, the best restaurant in Worcester.

It's no picnic raising three children alone, but she has made life very pleasant for her children and it shows in their actions. All three are very polite and thoughtful of others. She says, "They are twelve, ten and eight years old, going on forty, thirty and twenty. Here are some pictures of them for you." Their names are Sally, Mary and Toby. I always compliment Mary Jean on the great job she is doing with her kids. Through all of this she has managed to keep a positive outlook on life and has never allowed herself to become bitter.

#

The concierge at the Bancroft recommended the Putnam & Thurston's Restaurant when I ask him about a good place to eat. He gives me one of their menus before I go there for the first time, so I have some idea of what I want to order. They serve the best cuisine in New England. "It is fine dining at its best," I tell everyone.

The first time I visit the Restaurant, I am quite impressed with the decor. You enter to the right or to the left.

To the right is the door to the main dining room; and to the left is the door to the coffee shop and counter seating dining area.

Upon entering the main dining room there is a hatcheck room where Jo, the hatcheck lady, greets you. The men love Jo because when they leave, she helps them on with their coat; and as she holds the coat for them to slip into, she gives them a hug from behind. If they are a first-time customer, they are quite surprised when she does this to them. Every man who leaves Putman & Thurston's usually gives Jo a very nice tip and they always have a smile on their face.

There is a table centered under a large chandelier at the front of the dining room with a flowing fountain situated on the table.

To the right of the hatcheck area is the entrance to the cocktail lounge with seating for 75 to 80 people. In the rear of the bar is a small stage for a piano, where nightly music greets the patrons.

The dining room extends to the rear of the building approximately 100 feet where it spreads into a rectangular room with leather bound booths lining the three walls, with tables in the center.

The walls are lined with decorative wallpaper depicting pastoral scenes. There are Coach Lights on the wall at each booth, with beautiful chandeliers throughout the room.

The presentation on the tables consists of white linen table cloths and napkins with sterling silver sugar bowls and sterling silver capped salt and pepper shakers.

Between the formal dinning room and the coffee shop there are stairs that lead to the second floor where the office and banquet rooms are found.

The coffee shop is the length of the main dining room, ending where the rectangular area began. The kitchen is behind the coffee shop, adjacent to the dining room, with swinging doors to each area.

As I enter the coffee shop there is an area called "The Amen Corner", protected by a glass wall from the inside entry door, with several tables. From the corner is a leather bench for additional seating with tables and chairs placed perpendicular to the bench.

The kitchen is all electric and fully equipped with all stainless steel counters, and appliances. The floors are tiled. There are three stoves, two broilers and a double fryer.

The large banquet room on the second level has a capacity for 400 people. The smaller banquet room holds 125 people, with a cocktail lounge seating for 60 people.

The area between the coffee shop and the main dining room contains the cashier's desk with a glass display case with an assortment of chewing gum, cigarettes, and cigars. Across from the cashier's desk are the rest rooms. As I consume my first meal in the coffee shop I ponder my life and what has become of it. One day I was a young woman in college without a care in the world and here I am now, in deep 'Shineola'.

Chance and I have become friendly with one of the owners of Putnam & Thurston's. He is a very nice young man. He spent four years in the Army as a 1st Lieutenant, and with me being an Army brat and Chance with his stint in the Army, we all had a lot in common. His name is Spero Panos. Spero has a strong build, looks to be less than six feet tall. He isn't what I would call fat, but we can tell he enjoys the food he serves. He takes Chance and me on a tour of his restaurant one evening. We are very impressed with the decor and the elegance of the place.

Spero played semi-pro football for a while after College. He is very handsome and has a great personality. He always makes us feel like we are one of the family when we come to his restaurant. We go in on Friday evenings a lot to have their famous Special, 'Stuffed Broiled Lobster'. When Spero finds out that Chance is a gourmet cook, he gives him his secret to their famous, very tasty, lobster. He tells him, "You crush Ritz Crackers and pour melted butter over them, add a little salt, pepper and garlic powder and there you have it." It certainly didn't taste that simple. Their Stuffed Lobsters are the best lobsters I have ever eaten. Chance agrees.

#

Several months pass, Chance and I don't seem to have too much interference from, you-know-who. I have performed about 12 abortions. And I follow his orders to the letter.

I have been having nightmares about our operation and the "what if's". I woke up one morning in a cold sweat. I had a dream about finding Charles in a laboratory with a "Frankenstein" like figure that he was trying to bring to life. I don't dare tell Chance about my dreams; he will think I'm daft.

#

On Monday morning, a doctor phones me from one of the local hospitals. He identifies himself as Dr. Kendal and asks to have a meeting with me and insists it be kept confidential. Not knowing what this doctor has in store, I agree to meet with him the following morning. I suggest that he come to the clinic at 8:00 a. m., before anyone else arrives for the day.

On Tuesday morning, when Dr. James Kendal meets with me, he says, "I have a patient who is in poor health and in the final month of her pregnancy. She wants a 'Partial Birth Abortion', and I can't do that at our hospital. Would you consider doing it here?" Dr. Kendal continues, "We have a reputation to uphold at the hospital and we would not recover from the bad publicity." He continues, "I might add that this woman is very prominent in this community and you would be paid very handsomely."

"So, let me get this straight, you want to protect the good name of your hospital, but you don't care about the reputation of my Clinic, seeing as how we already perform abortions. Is that the core of this conversation?"

"Well, I wouldn't put it that way, doctor," as his face reddens.

"Oh really Doctor? Just how would you put murder?"

He starts to sputter, "Well, I mean, you already do abortions. We don't, so what would be the problem?"

"The problem, Dr. Kendal, is that we may do abortions, but we do not do live births and then kill the baby," I said with a stern voice. "Do I look like a 'Barbarian' to you, Doctor?" "Now get the hell out of my clinic and tell the big shots at your perfect hospital, that the answer is NO. And I don't care how much money this woman has, I don't murder babies."

Dr. Kendal comes back with, "Well, what ever happened to professional courtesy?"

"I don't call this professional courtesy, Doctor, I call this disgusting. Good Bye, Doctor." I hold the door open and with a hand signal, I show him the daylight.

As he walks out the door he turns and says, "I hope you never need a favor, Doctor, because if you ever do, don't come to me."

"I'll make a note of that," I say with disgust in my voice, as I slammed the door in his face. I mutter to myself as I walk back to my office, "What a jerk...the nerve of that guy...for this I got up an hour early this morning."

I didn't tell Chance about that jerk. He would probably have given him a well deserved, sound whipping.

Chapter IX

MEETING CORA

The replacement for the other doctor who left the clinic is a woman in her mid 40's. Her name is Dr. Cora Beasley, and she is as stern as her appearance. I could tell she is ex-military, without even asking, just by the way she carries herself, very erect posture and a stern and purposeful walk. Cora is a very imposing woman. She has very short-cropped hair, almost mannish. She is about 5 feet 8 inches tall, with a corpulent build. She rather reminds me of the Matrons you see in those 'B' movies about women's Prisons. She has a brusque manner about her. Cora and I get along well; which comes as a surprise to me, as Cora is very intimidating when you first meet her. I want to dislike her because of who she works for; but for some reason I just can't. She is a very endearing person. As the months go by we become closer than I ever would have anticipated.

As we are on a coffee break one afternoon the conversation turns to Cora as she expounds on her philosophy toward men and how she chose a life in the Military. "Men have a problem with me. They don't seem to know how to handle me, so they just stay away. I guess its okay. I've never had time to play men's silly games anyway." Cora says, "I attended College at the University of Minnesota, majoring in medicine and was in ROTC. I went into the Army for an eight-year stint. I left the army with the rank of Lieutenant Colonel then entered the Minnesota School of Medicine and interned at the University Medical Center Hospital."

Cora is an excellent doctor. Despite her military training, she is a marshmallow in a Doberman's suit. Cora, Mary Jean, and I become known as the 'three Musketeers'.

This actually bothers me because I am torn between being loyal to our cause and enjoying the friendship of the enemy. I think, *how awful, I really like Cora, and I'm going to have to destroy her reputation. Why did she have to work for that awful Charles?*

Cora grew up in Albert Lea, Minnesota. She says, "I was raised in a family of 12 children. I went into the Military because I was so used to being in a regimented environment that I thought it was the right thing for me. I dearly loved Army life, but I love medicine more; and eight years in the Military was plenty for me."

Cora continues, "My parents are both gone now and my siblings are spread all over the country. We keep in touch with each other through taped recordings. One will start the recording; mail it to the next one; they will record something and mail it on to the next sibling, and so on. Sometimes they put pictures of their kids to keep us up on their growing bigger and bigger. By the time it all gets to me, I can listen to the goings-on of everyone's life, happenings etc, and see their faces. I then record my events onto the tape and send it on to one of the others. When one tape is full, someone starts a new one. The tapes are then numbered, put in a large envelope and mailed to the next sibling. It just goes on and on. It is a wonderful way to communicate; it's cheaper than trying to talk to everyone by phone; and everyone gets a chance to make their statement, tell their news and show off their kids. When each tape is finished and everyone has had a chance to hear it, it is sent to the oldest sibling and he stores it with the others for posterity."

Cora adds, "I can hardly wait for each shipment of tapes. When they arrive, I'll bring them to the Clinic and share them with you." We all start looking forward to the arrival of the tapes. As each sibling talks, Cora shows us pictures of that person and tells about what they were like as a child. One day Cora received a Videotape of three of her siblings and their families frolicking at a park. Cora was overcome with emotion. She watched it over and over until she almost wore it out. She sent it on to another sibling after she had a copy made.

I tell Chance of my anxiety over my friendship with Cora and how I will have to destroy our friendship when this is all over.

"I truly like her Chance, she is such a good person." I confide to him.

Chance says, "Oh, don't worry too much about it. I'm sure everything will turn out okay."

"But we get along so great. How am I going to turn on a friend? I am really upset about this Chance," I confess.

Chance continues, "Perhaps you should try staying away from her for a while. Be less friendly, maybe."

"That will be very hard, but I'll try."

Chance says, "This entire ordeal is taking a toll on you." He comforts me as best he can, but there is just nothing he can say or do right now to convince me that everything will work out okay.

Chance tells me, "Everything will all work out in the end, you'll see." He gives me a hug and a pat on the back. I sense he is keeping something from me, but as an Army brat, I am used to not asking questions.

Chapter X

THE COMPOUND

I haven't had an opportunity to cook for Chance yet but I find out just what a great cook he is. He's a natural. You would think you were in a fancy restaurant in New York City. As it turns out we have quite a few meals together. We make a contest out of who can out-cook the other. Cooking is great therapy; it cuts down on the stress we are under.

Cooking is one of my talents. I have one dish, however, that I like, but just can't seem to make it work, so I exchange recipes with Chance and we have a contest to see who can best improve on each other's recipe. Chance also has a recipe that he has trouble with.

Chance wins; he makes my dish taste exactly like when the Chef made it. The recipe is called "Turkey a la Veau". I got the recipe from a Chef I watched at a Home Show several years ago. I say, "I am frantically writing down the ingredients as he is talking and demonstrating, but when I made it, it just didn't taste quite the same."

Chance said, "The ingredients you left out of the recipe was lemon juice and lemon and orange zest. You had all the other good things in there but that is the final flavor that does the trick."

"Thanks Chance," I say. "I was writing the ingredients down so fast, I guess I forgot the most important ones." I add, "I was convinced that he added an ingredient when no one was looking and neglected to tell us about it. Isn't it amazing how something so simple can make or break a recipe?"

"It sure is," Chance says, "I learned that the hard way in culinary school."

I am very thankful that I will be able to make this dish and enjoy it, because I loved it when I tasted it at the Home Show.

With A Wink And A Nod

#

Chance and I have another of our famous "cook-offs" at his place. It is his turn to put on the feedbag. "Marvelous meal, Chance," I exclaim. He makes Cornish Game Hens, stuffed with Wild Rice, in a wine sauce. "Bravo! Bravo!" I yell, as I applaud the meal.

"Thank you, Thank you ma'am for that ovation," he comes back, with an English flare and a bow.

"You know what I think, Chance?" "I think we should open a restaurant. We would knock them dead with our recipes." "Oops, I guess that was the wrong choice of words," I said.

"Not a bad idea. Not bad at all," Chance says as he has a contemplating look on his face.

Chance has just returned from his trip to Bethesda, where he visited with Charles. He went back to the Facility in Bethesda for a few days to see what he can come up with. Chance has an 'in' with the Higher-ups, more so than I. He says, "I will nose around to see if I can possibly find out just where the experiments are taking place."

"I found out all right," He says, "It's in a desolate area in the mountains of Wyoming. I believe the only access will be by Helicopter, from what I can see of the area. This is an area that looks to have been unvisited by humans, not only because of its ruggedness, but because it looks to be impenetrable." Chance adds, "But it can't be too isolated if Charles has the lab there. He has to get in somehow."

Chance says, "I took pictures of a map on the wall in Charles' office. There is an indication where this isolated area is to be found. Anyone not knowing about the project would have no suspicions about the map, as Charles has land in Wyoming, and often speaks of how beautiful the area is. Charles almost caught me taking the pictures. One more second and I would have had a lot of explaining to do."

Chance says, "I visited Charles in his office in the guise of giving him a progress report on the preparations for the project. Charles gets called away for a few minutes and I took advantage of the private moment to take pictures of the map. Charles came back just as I put the camera back in my coat pocket. I pretended to be looking for a stick of gum."

Chance and I have to discuss our next move, which is to find out more about the operation. We examine the photos of the map. "A little hard to see any details, don't you think?" I ask.

"Let's have the pictures blown up at the One Hour Photo Shop down the street." Once that is accomplished, we can really make out the details of the area.

Chance is right. No one would be popping in on them there. It is hidden deep in the Rocky Mountains, on a government owned section near Gros Ventre Range. We can see how the only way in would probably be by Helicopter, or perhaps on foot.

"What we need now is a pilot." I mutter.

"Ah, my lady, fret no more, you are looking at one," Chance quips.

"Chance, you never cease to amaze me." I wanted to throw my arms around his neck but I restrained myself.

Chance says, "I have had a fascination with flying since childhood. I have an Uncle Norman, who was a bomber pilot in World War II. Whenever Uncle Norman came to Osage he would take me up in his airplane for a spin around the countryside."

"Uncle Norman lived in Omaha, Nebraska. He had his own plane and chartered flights to Canada for big corporate fishing trips. I grew to love flying. We would fly over my house and my mother would be working in her garden. As we flew over the house, Norman would tip his wings as a signal to Mother. She would pick up her hoe and wave it at us."

Chance continues, "I learned to fly while I was in Vietnam. One of my Army buddies, Wayne Jensten, was a pilot and during our down time in Vietnam he would take me out for flying lessons. I kept up my flying after my discharge and went on to get my Pilots license. I have logged quite a few hours, and now I have my own plane."

"After I got out of the Army," Chance says, "I was 27 years old; so I went to Medical School on the GI Bill. I was in ROTC in College at the University of Iowa, and went into the Army as an Officer."

"I went to Medical School at the University of Virginia, in Charlottesville. This is where I met Alma. We were married right after graduation. It wasn't too much of a struggle for us money wise, because Alma's family had money and I was going to school courtesy of the taxpayers. I had my own money, but at that time it was tied up in a Trust Fund."

"It's the least this country can do for the boys who protect our freedoms," I said. "Sometimes this country doesn't do enough for our servicemen. So far as I am concerned; they should have a free ride for school, medical, housing and business for the rest of their lives for what they do for our country, especially those who are maimed for life. But then that would really boost the Income Taxes out of sight, wouldn't it?"

"If our taxes were going for our military men instead of all the wasteful special interests, I wouldn't mind so much. It just galls me to have to pay for everyone else's stupidity or greed. Unless you are in a wheelchair or on crutches and can't work you should not be on welfare. If the government would stop subsidizing illegitimate children perhaps there would be fathers in the homes instead of single mothers with three, four and five children that our taxes are paying for."

Chance agrees and continues to tell me about his family, "I grew up in the small town of Osage, Iowa. My mother died of a heart attack when she was 46 years old, and my father died five years later of an aneurysm. He was 51. I've been on my own since I was 17. I've always been independent. Mother taught me to take care of myself. She would say to me, "Chauncey, God gave you two hands, two feet, and one brain, use all of them to help the less fortunate and use them for a betterment of mankind. Don't injure with your hands. Don't step on anyone's pride. And always think before you act." She was a wise woman."

Chance is quite brilliant. He tells me, "I graduated from High School at age 17. I entered college and took some pre-med courses. I discovered that I liked medicine and elected to go into the Medical field after my stint in the Army."

"My father worked hard all his life as a homebuilder. He built the home in which I grew up. It was so sturdy, a tornado couldn't touch it. A tornado came through Osage one time and our house was the only one standing on the entire block. And, of course, Dad had to jump in and help everyone rebuild. Still, to this day, I don't know if he actually charged anyone for his service."

One time the jail was on fire and we all ran to watch. Dad ran to help. Firemen hacked at window bars while flames licked at their ladders. The firemen moved shadow-like about their solemn duties as flames outlined their figures. As flames swept upward the scene became one of horror. Several prisoners died in that fire along with three guards.

"Dad was a tall imposing man with black hair, and a year round tan from working out-doors all his adult life. He was a very serious man and believed in hard work. He would tell me, 'Chauncey, if a man isn't a hard worker, he isn't worth his salt.' He taught me the ins and outs of the construction business. I can probably build my own house if I ever have the time. I worked for Dad every summer from when I was 10 years old until he passed away. His younger brother, Clarence, took over the construction business after Dad died."

"I always marveled at how my father could chuck down two aspirin without the aid of any liquid. I guess when you are on top of a roof and you get a headache, you just don't have time to go back to the ground for some water. He always carried aspirin with him because he would get horrible tension headaches and if he didn't catch it quickly they would linger for hours," Chance explains. "As a doctor, I now know how dangerous it is to take aspirin without water."

Chance also talks about his mother, Penny, "She was tall and slender. Her hobby was gardening. She furnished fresh vegetables to just about everyone in Osage, during the summer. She belonged to the Garden Club and won several Blue Ribbons at the County Fair for her vegetables and her famous Carrot Cake. What we didn't eat or can we gave away to others except her Carrot Cake recipe. She made the cake for every holiday. Her secret was her home grown carrots," Chance brags. "I inherited the recipe after she died, and I carry on the same tradition of making the cake for every holiday."

"Carrot Cake is one of my favorites."

Chance talks about his sister with much sadness in his voice. "She was six years older than I. She died of pneumonia when she was seven years old. There was a creek near our home and she and some of the neighbor kids were playing near it. She slipped in and got soaking wet. She knew she wasn't supposed to play near the creek so she didn't go home until her clothes dried off. The accident occurred on a chilly autumn day and she became ill the next day. I was only one year old and I don't remember her. I have pictures of her that Mother would show me and tell me about her. Her name was Gloria."

Chance continues, "Mother told me Gloria was always very frail and sickly. After that dip in the creek she just wasn't strong enough to fight off Pneumonia. Gloria had Diabetes also."

I notice that when Chance talks about his mother and father he has a lot of pride in his voice; but when he talks about Gloria, he becomes very distressed. It is almost as if he wants to remember her as flesh and blood rather than just a figure in a photo. He has always kept the photos of his sister and he showed them to me. The photos showed that she was indeed a frail little girl, with the face of an angel.

"After the deaths of my parents," Chance says, "I inherited a large fortune. It was put in a Trust Fund, which I could not touch until I was 30 years old. I took the money out of the Trust Fund when I turned 31 and invested it in Bonds and Mutual Funds, which have made me even wealthier. At age 31, I finished Medical School and went into my own private practice back in Osage. Several years later I was asked to join the staff at the Bethesda Facility to work on research for the government. I jumped at the chance to do research. I always had in the back of my mind that some day I or someone would find a cure for Diabetes."

"That would be fabulous if someone found a cure for that disease and about a dozen others that have been around for centuries."

Chance nods and continues, "I started a Foundation for Research on Children's Diabetes. I named the Fund after my sister. All the Interest I earn from my securities goes into the Foundation. I have several old friends from high school, whom I trust, to run the foundation for me. I check in with them periodically in case they need advice on something; otherwise the foundation is run quite smoothly."

"You have had a fascinating life, Chance. A person wouldn't know you were that wealthy. At least I had no idea you were that wealthy. My family has money, but not enough to start a foundation."

"Wealth is wonderful, Laura, if you use it properly. I was always taught to use my brain and my wealth to help others."

"You certainly have the right idea, Chance." Again, I wanted to throw my arms around him and give him a huge hug. <u>I don't know why I keep hesitating about that hug.</u>

Chapter XI

SEPARATE FLIGHTS

The following weekend, Chance and I take a little trip. I take Friday off from the clinic so we have plenty of time to travel and accomplish what has to be done. We are always very careful not to be seen together too much, so we go to the Airport in separate taxis, at separate times and take separate flights. The Worcester Airport is very small and we fly out in twin-engine planes. I fly to Boston and then to Wyoming. Chance flies to New York and then on to Wyoming. We do this just in case Charles or his people are watching us. I think we are a little paranoid. You get that way when you work for the government for any length of time.

This is why we usually eat in, instead of going to restaurants too often. That way if we are seen going to each other's resident, it will look like we are having a meeting. We want to make sure Charles doesn't catch on to what we are really doing. When we do go to a Restaurant, we make sure our conversations are kept very light and business-like.

Chance has both of our living quarters swept with electronic 'debugging' devices. We make sure to hire a Private Detective who has absolutely no ties to the government. We never discuss anything over the phone, other than what time we will meet. "Don't ever underestimate the government and their ways of not trusting anyone," Chance says. "I guess we are overdoing it sometimes, but we are so desperate to blow the whistle on this project, we are not going to do anything to jeopardize it," he adds.

Our flights take us to Casper, Wyoming. We rent a van and motor to a small community near Riverton, where Chance's old Army buddy lives, who will lend him his helicopter, no questions asked.

His name is **Wayne Jensten**. He is quite the character. He lives like a mountain man. It appears as if he hasn't shaved in 20 years. He has black hair and a red beard. He seems to be very smart, but quite nervous.

The area, where he lives, is enveloped with Aspen and Pine trees and wild berry bushes. Mountains skirt the area with their majestic power. I breathe in the perfume of the clean air and feel the serenity all around me. I have never lived in the mountains, but I think I could spend my whole life in a place like this.

I take a liking to Wayne right away. There is just something about him that makes him very likable. As Chance introduces him to me I feel a strong handshake as I look into the deep brown eyes of this six-foot tall man. Mountains surround his cabin. I don't ask, but I'm willing to bet that he built the cabin himself. He has a generator that provides electricity for his lights and refrigeration. He has installed Solar Panels on the south side of the cabin for emergency heating and electricity during the bitter cold and cloudy winter months. He also has a beautiful fireplace where he has rigged a contraption so he can roast fresh kill or cook a pot of soup or stew. He says, "I had to learn how to cook, because I have been on my own for about 20 years." He has a pot of stew cooking when Chance and I arrive. He also has a wood burning stove inside the cabin.

"This is delicious," I exclaim, "What's in it?"

"It's Elk meat and wild vegetables that grow in the mountains," Wayne answers. "There are all sorts of vegetables that grow in these mountains. You can find wild onions, wild garlic, turnips, asparagus, chives, and, if you know what to look for, herbs such as sage, thyme and rosemary." Wayne adds, "You can usually smell the herbs before you even see them if they are growing in a large patch."

I ask, "How did they get there, Wayne?"

"I don't know for sure, but I have heard stories about how the Indians planted them many years ago and they just keep coming up. Some years there are more than other years. I think they probably grow good one year and sparse the next, sort of the way wild apples, grapes, and strawberries grow," Wayne explains. "I make apple pie and apple sauce from the wild apples and wine from the wild grapes. You're drinking my homemade wine now. And, of course, who doesn't like strawberry short cake once in a while."

"Oh, wow," I said, "I was wondering where you got this wonderful wine way out here in the wilderness; you should bottle this stuff, you could make a fortune. I agree with you about the strawberries. I could eat them all day long."

Chance says, "Me too, I love strawberries. I don't think I have ever eaten a wild strawberry before; the flavor is amazing and I was just going to ask if there was a Winery around here."

"No. . .no Winery, just me, the little old wine maker," Wayne says, with a big grin. He adds, "I suppose when the 'White Man' invaded their territory, the Indians just pulled up stakes and moved on and left all the fruit, vegetables and herbs to grow wild. I think perhaps they didn't give much thought to digging everything up and taking it with them. I'm sure they must have taken a few plants and perhaps some seedlings; but they probably didn't have time to take all of it. I'm also sure that they probably had to leave in a hurry; as the white man was moving in on them. From what I have heard, they were a very private and shy people." Wayne continues, "I think perhaps the Indians who were around here were the Salish Tribe. They were a little-known Tribe out of Montana, more commonly known as Flatheads. There have been signs around of their presence. They were into different herbs and they grew more food than the other tribes. That's why they think the Salish people once lived around here."

"They sure must have planted hearty seeds, for it to keep coming up like this," Chance mentions.

Wayne thinks for a while and says, "Well, they had the original stuff in those days, not the hybrids we have now. I think sometimes, they eliminate a lot of hearty goodness from seeds, when they start altering them."

"Gee, I wish we had time, I would love to go hunting for the herbs and vegetables," I said.

"The next time you're here, we will do just that, Laura," Wayne promises.

"This is the first time I have ever tasted Elk meat and I really like it in this stew with all those great wild veggies."

Wayne says, "I go into town once a month for my staples, otherwise I pretty much keep to myself and live mainly off the land."

Chance and Wayne talked a long time that night, mostly about their times together in the army. I was happy to just sit and listen to their great tales from their army days. They seem to be able to start up where they left off the last time they saw each other. Wayne has a wonderful sense of humor. We almost talk and laugh the night away. We didn't get to bed until around 2:30 in the morning.

The next morning Wayne has breakfast all cooked and waiting for us. The aroma of bacon, eggs and coffee wakens us. Wayne has a small hut behind his cabin where he houses a few chickens. He says, "I butcher them once in a while and replace them with chicks that I buy when I go into town." The cabin is a lot bigger than it looks from the outside. He has three bedrooms, a kitchen, with an eating area, and a very large living room, plus two bathrooms. "I'm close enough to the city so I can be on the city sewer system. And I'm just far enough away that I'm not bothered by city ordinances. I have the best of both worlds out here."

Wayne says, "I like the extra bedrooms because sometimes I take vacationers out into the mountains to camp or hunt. Sometimes they spend the night at the cabin before they go on their mountain hikes. I enjoy the company but wouldn't want to do it all the time. I have a few pilot friends who usually come to visit and spend the night also."

Wayne has gone out to tend to his morning chores. After we are fed and dressed, Wayne drives us to the Riverton Airport. This is where he keeps his helicopter. I am very surprised when I see it. It is immaculate. Wayne is very fastidious when it comes to his helicopter.

He keeps it in tip-top condition because he never knows when he will need it for an emergency; and it needs to be in good working condition when he wants to hop in and take off at a moments notice. He says, "I do all the mechanics on the helicopter, not that I don't trust anyone, but I want to make sure everything is right, in my own mind. The only way to do that is to do it myself. About three times a week I go to the Airport and clean, polish, and repair anything that needs repairing. I oil, re-oil, check, and re-check everything. I double-check every nut and bolt. I am very meticulous about my home and my helicopter. Sometimes there is an emergency with a hiker in the mountains. They fall and injure themselves, or fall down a ravine. When the word goes out, I get in my Chopper and go for the rescue. The mountains are beautiful, but they are also treacherous if you don't know the area."

Now, I have never been in a helicopter in my life. This isn't something that a person does every day. I'm very frightened and the guys can tell. I am getting a little green around the gills. Chance explains that there is nothing to it. "I will keep it as steady as I can, but in the mountains, it can get a little hairy with the down drafts and up drafts."

Well, that certainly didn't make me feel any better, I think to myself. Chance explains, "The helicopter makes its own wind, so the down drafts and up drafts don't really bother it so much. I just want you to be aware of what to expect in a helicopter."

They are having a good chuckle at my expense, I thought. I'm a 'white knuckle' passenger for about the first half hour. Once I get used to it, it really isn't so bad. I'm glad I came. It also helps to know that I can trust the pilot.

Chance is a very confident pilot and he isn't the type to show off for my benefit. In fact he is very careful not to make any sudden turns without warning me beforehand. I am grateful that he is considerate of my uneasiness. I guess if you have been flying as long as Chance has, it just comes as second nature for you. I become more and more at ease as the flight goes on. I am certainly enjoying this fabulous view of the mountains and all of God's creation. It amazes me how nature takes care of itself; it replants itself after a fire and restores itself after man has taken what he wants.

Chance purchases a very expensive camera to take pictures of the area. It is my duty to take the pictures while Chance keeps that bird in the air. I have always been fascinated with photography. I took a course in Photography while in college. I even belonged to the Photography Club. I learned to look for details for my shots. I take some fantastic pictures of the area. Chance gets as close as he can to the Project. People are used to seeing helicopters in these areas, as they are usually looking for lost hikers. The camera has a high-powered zoom so we can be far enough away and still get close-up pictures.

The Compound is in the most isolated area that we have ever seen. It is a lot larger than we imagined. There is enough space for a small town. I can't make out any details at first, but then something very strange catches my eye. "Chance, hold it steady. I think I see something. I can make out a waterfall and what looks like a small rain forest under an enormous Bubble. I'll bet that the bubble must be where the occupants are living. I think it must be made out of glass because I see it is very shinny, or perhaps an acrylic of some kind. The sun is reflecting off of the south side, can you see it"? "Wait, I think they are solar panels on the south side of the bubble. Wow, let me zoom in a little more. They are definitely solar panels, as the sun reflects off something large and shiny. I am getting some great shots, Chance. Try to hold it a little steadier. Great, that did it. Oh my, Chance, this is big, I'm talking really big. How in the world did they get all this stuff up here without anyone seeing them?" I ask?

"Good question, Laura. And yes, I can see the sun's reflection. I wish I had an answer for you, I have no idea what that could be; it sure looks like glass or an acrylic surface. Get several shots of that one." Chance replies.

"You've got it." I reply.

We only have half an hours worth of fuel left, so Chance turns and heads for the Airport. I'm awe struck at what I see. Chance is very silent on the way back. After we land he looks at me and says, "I'm very frightened for the first time since we started this sabotage mission."

"Why", I ask.

He hesitates and then says, "This is so much bigger than I expected. We are going to need more help on this. I'm sure you will see it in the photos that you took, but I think you were so into taking the pictures you didn't see what I saw," he said. "Laura, I saw some big artillery down there. I saw an artillery hut outside of the see through bubble and what looked like a canon sticking out of it. This place is highly fortified and very difficult to get to. Did you see any roads or paths? Do you understand what this means?"

I am having so much fun playing the 'Nancy Drew' bit that I don't even think about the repercussions of this whole thing. All of a sudden, I begin to sweat, and it wasn't that warm in the mountains. "I understand what you mean. Oh, Chance, what are we going to do? I think there is some kind of pathway, but there were too many trees and brush to get a full picture. What have we gotten ourselves into? How are we going to expose a project this huge?" I ask.

"I have an idea," he said, "I just need to work out some details and hope everything will fall into place."

Something tells me not to ask any more questions. . .at least not at this time. My background taught me not to ask questions. Being around my father and some of his highly covert missions that he went on, I wait for information to be given instead of pumping people for information. I learned to have faith in a person's decisions. In the back of my mind I know Chance will come through with the right answers when the time is right.

When we get back to Wayne's cabin, Chance confides in him. Wayne is more than eager to join us in our quest. He said, "I've waited 20 years to get back at the government for what they did to me. Do you think I chose to live like a hermit in this desolate area of Wyoming?"

Chance says, "I hadn't really given it much thought. I just presumed that after your breakup with Rose, you just decided to shun society and live alone."

Wayne tells us, "I was flying a secret mission during the Vietnam War. I was to dump a load of bombs on a site near Dong Hoi in North Vietnam. It was a night mission, so we wouldn't be detected; and then get out of the area and back to the base in Saigon. The site was an area where the North Vietnamese kept their ammo supply depot. This particular supply depot was the largest one they had and where they stored most of their weaponry and ammunition."

Wayne continued, "I radioed back to the base that it was a direct hit. I said the explosion lit up the sky for a half hour. I told them it looked like the Fourth of July. I was proud of my success on that mission. To throw us off, and not wanting their adversaries to find out they lost most of their weaponry and ammo supply, the North Vietnamese released a news report that said, 'A small village of innocent women and children was wiped out by American bombs.' Before the Army could stifle the story, the American Press got hold of it and went crazy reporting it to the United States as a big blunder. By the time the news got back to the U.S., it got blown all out of proportion and the "bleeding hearts" leaped all over the government for it. When the liberal Media gets hold of something, they never let go until they have milked it bone dry. It was the Media that gave that war a bad name. Perhaps some day it will all backfire and the Media will have to start being accountable for their actions."

Wayne pauses and shakes his head, "As a result of this propaganda, the government spread the word that an Army pilot got his orders mixed up and bombed the wrong area. After all, the Army, in their own unique way, wasn't about to take the blame for any wrong doing, even though they knew it was all a purposeful fabrication."

Wayne continues, "I took the fall for the whole mess so the Army wouldn't get a 'black eye'. Hence, I lost my Rose, my wonderful Rose. The strain of going through all that shame was just too much for her; and I was sworn to keep the army's secret. I couldn't even tell my Rose."

I left the Army in "disgrace". That's the way they put it and I almost had a nervous breakdown. The Army is forced to give me a dishonorable discharge and send me on my way. They did, however, secretly hand me a large envelope of money to get me started in a new life and to keep my mouth shut. I worked at several jobs, none of which satisfied me. I was able to buy my own helicopter and this gave me more satisfaction than anything else. I have lived in these mountains ever since."

Wayne walks over to Chance, gives him a hug and says, "Thanks brother, I'll do anything you ask me to do...anything."

At this point Chance asks me if I would mind if he speaks to Wayne in private. I am rather puzzled by this, but do not question his motives.

I say, "I think I will take a shower while you two talk."

"Thanks, Laura," Chance says.

It is rather a touching moment for Chance and Wayne. Chance does not offer any explanation for wanting to speak to Wayne alone, so I keep silent about it. (I'm to find out soon enough just what their conversation is about.)

After my shower I get dressed and walk outside. This mountain air is fantastic. I take a deep breath and exhale slowly. As I view the area I sense there is something or someone watching me. I turn slowly and sure enough there is a bear cub looking at me. He is probably wondering what I'm doing there. I restrain myself from walking up to him as I have heard about mama bears and how protective they are of their young. I take a few steps back and feel for the door knob and slowly open the door and slip in as fast as I can without disturbing the cub.

I here Chance say, "Are you okay, Laura?"

"Yes Chance, I just had a visit with a bear cub and I quietly slipped back into the cabin before the mother showed up."

The next morning we say good bye to Wayne and back to the air port to catch our flights home. I give Wayne a big hug and thank him for his hospitality.

Chapter XII

BACK TO REALITY

I arrive at the clinic early Monday morning. I have a lot of thinking to do, and to try to make some sense of all this. I haven't heard from Chance since we left each other at the Worcester Airport. He told me he was going to lay low for a while, that he has some planning to think about.

#

What I didn't know, at that time, is that he is chasing down a few old buddies from his unit in the Army. I discover that Chance and his buddies have a very close bond between them, more so than most ex-GI's. They are closer than any other group of men who served in the war together. I am amazed at how they have stayed in touch all these years.

Chance told me, "We were thrown into a very bloody and controversial war. We keep in touch and whenever anyone needs one of the others for support or anything else, we are there for each other." There is a reason for their closeness, a very good reason; one to which I am introduced when the time comes.

#

One by one, Chance contacts each one of his buddies. There are 22 of them in all, counting Chance. How they all survived the Vietnam War, is a wonder in itself. Chance says, "This group of men saw more than their share of combat."

Chance is trying to figure out how he is going to house all these guys when they finally get together. He thinks of a plan to put them up in different Hotels and Motels around the City. That way, if they are being followed, it will take an army to keep up with them. I tell Chance that I would help pay for their rooms if there is a problem with finances. I don't want him footing the entire bill and I didn't expect these loyal, great guys to pay their own way. Chance says, "It won't be necessary, as they are all businessmen and they have plenty of their own money. Thanks for your concern and consideration. That is very kind of you."

Fourteen of the men and some of their wives show up in Worcester a week later. They stagger their arrivals so as not to draw too much attention to themselves.

Some of the other men were ill or just simply unable to come because of a previous commitment. No one ever questions the other as to his reason for not showing up, or his reason to show up. It is an unspoken bond, one that not too many people will ever see between this many men and their wives. They work as one and they think as one when they are together.

Chance introduces me to the men and their wives, a few at a time. They don't want to be too conspicuous in their meetings. I meet some of them at Putnam & Thurston's. Chance has me meet him there. He is with two of his buddies and one of their wives.

The first person I am introduced to is **Bobby Joe Caldwell**; his expertise is blowing things up. He talks about dynamite as if it is a beautiful woman. "I have a respect for explosives and I know the ins and outs of every aspect of them. I know what makes this one or that one volatile." The way he handles plastics scares me to death until I find out plastics are harmless until an electrical impulse is introduced. As I enter the restaurant, I see this well built tall blond haired man stand up to greet me. He has a face you might see in Gentlemen's Quarterly magazine. I observe his very prominent, chiseled features. Chance explains, "He didn't bring his wife, because she had to stay home in Dallas, Texas, to keep an eye on their business and their four children. Bobby Joe and Doreen own a dynamite and drilling materials company." Bobby Joe is the type of person you want to have in your life. He is kind, thoughtful, respectful, and just an all around nice guy. He loves to eat, although you wouldn't know it to look at him.

The next couple I meet sitting at the table is **Chip Dagget**, and his wife **Trudy**. Chip, very politely, stands to greet me. Climbing is Chip's qualification. Chip's red hair and beard stand out like a neon sign. Trudy is Chip's partner in every sense of the word. They are experts at hang-gliding. Trudy is small in build with a very sweet and friendly face. Chance introduces them and says, "They live in Pueblo, Colorado, where they have a mountain climbing and camping equipment store. They will furnish the equipment we will need for our trip to Wyoming."

Several days later they take some of the men and go to a gym to practice their climbing skills. Chance says, "Trudy is small but mighty. She doesn't appear to be the athletic type, but she can out climb most men." I find Trudy to be a very genuine person. If she takes a liking to you she is your friend for life. Chip has the type of personality that you don't see too often in people today. He loves helping people. He is always the first to volunteer for any mission. "I love an adventure." He tells the group.

All Chance's friends agree that this is one of the finest restaurants at which they have ever eaten. I get to know these people very quickly and feel as if I have known them all my life.

I remember that Chance is a stickler for detail; and we are all very grateful to him for that, as we find his details save our lives. I never gave this much thought when we worked at the Institute, because everyone concentrated on details there. Chance is like this with every thing he does in life. We go over and over every aspect of our strategy until it is clear in everyone's mind exactly what he or she has to do. Each one of the men has his own expertise and this is what Chance uses in assigning tasks to which they are best suited.

I dated a police officer for a while in college. He introduced me to guns and we would go to the shooting range about three times a week. I became a crack shot. "Thank you Tom Bergs, where ever you may be," I boast. Chance finds this very intriguing because he says, "I don't care much for guns, even though I am a marksman; but I have a lot of respect for them." Chance was a Captain in the Army, in charge of a Bravo Company located near the enemy lines.

Chapter XIII

MORE ARRIVALS

I cook a dinner for Bobby Joe and some of the others. Bobby just keeps on eating until everything is gone. He is a bottomless pit. We sure don't have to worry about leftovers when Bobby Joe is around. The other guests are a couple of old pals who have been together since childhood.

Milton Jones, (everyone calls him Uncle Miltie) says, "I was a gunner in the Vietnam War. I'm considered a sharpshooter. They say I can wipe out a sniper from a half-mile off; not really, but very close." He proves, several times, just how valuable he is as he saves a few of our lives before this is all over. Chance remembers a time or two when Uncle Miltie came to his rescue during the war. Every one of these men has his specialty and every one is an expert and takes great pride in his abilities. Milton tells about his best friend, **Willie Meehan,** as he motions his head toward him. "We have a Boat and Fishing business plus a Seafood Restaurant. We rent out boats and take groups out on Deep Sea fishing trips. We live in St. Petersburg, Florida. Our wives run the Seafood Restaurant."

When I first meet Uncle Miltie I sense that he is a sweet man and very strong. He acts tough, but I find out he is very soft hearted. He has a sort of crustiness about him and does not apologize when he cusses in front of a woman. He and his partner are in their mid fifties. Uncle Miltie is of average height, and he keeps in shape. His gray curly hair is an asset to his good looks. Most of the others in the group are in their forties.

Uncle Miltie always has a smile on his face. It amazes me how fourteen men can stop their lives and come together for a cause and never miss a beat. You would think these men had been together for the past 20 years, 24-7. They almost think as one mind. Sometimes I will see Chance look at one of the men and **with a *wink* and a *nod*** they seem to know what the other is thinking without saying a word.

In my mind I am thinking that there is something more to these men than what I am being told. How can this many men and their wives be so tuned in to each other's thoughts? They all seem to be on the same wavelength. Have I missed something?

William Meehan, Willie, accompanies Uncle Miltie. He is quite skilled with weapons also. Willie is just the opposite of Miltie. He is quiet; however, when he does say something, it is usually very profound. Two of Milton's boys are in their 20's and they help out in the business. Willie says, "My oldest child is a girl and she helps her mother and Milton's wife run our restaurant."

Willie is taller than Miltie. His coal black hair and massive build make him a very impressive man. Uncle Miltie and Willie are best friends and have been most of their lives. Willie tells us their story, "We grew up together, went into the Army together, and fought in Vietnam together and married sisters. We bought our houses next door to each other and went into business together. Friends just don't get any closer than this. A harsh word has never been spoken between us." As he talks, he looks at Miltie and gives him a soft punch on his burly arm. "Ain't that right, buddy?"

Uncle Miltie makes a fist as if he is going to knock Willie out and punches the air. "That's right pal, but just watch your step." He says with a smirk on his round smiling face. Willie and Miltie may be the oldest men of the team; however, they both are in excellent shape and can probably out perform the younger men.

Miltie adds, "Our wives are more than just our wives. They are our partners. We do everything together. We raise our kids together and we are in business together." For the most part the wives of the other men take care of the books for the business. The men handle the rest of it because most of them have gun shops or are in some part of the munitions business. A few of them are in the service business; like the next couple.

As I serve dessert **Steve and Joanne Gordon** sit very close to each other and seem to share a chuckle as Milton and Willie exchange gibes. Steve says, "I am a climber and hang-glider. Joanne and I own a ski lodge in the Rocky Mountains in Wyoming, near the Wind River Indian Reservation. Our Lodge will become our headquarters for our mission."

Joanne says, "Steve loves to putter, and is a Jack-Of-All trades. He can handle just about anything. If it needs building, he can build it. If it is broken, he can fix it." Steve is a big man, average height, and looks to weigh about 270 pounds. Joanne has a slight build and almost taller than Steve, a good woman with a heart of gold.

The next day I meet **Toni and Carol Rinaldi.** Toni doesn't have much to do until we all get to Wyoming. He works his tail off then. When it comes to flying, Toni is an ACE. Toni says, "Carol also loves to fly. She doesn't have her Pilots license yet, but she knows her way around an airplane. Once she gets her license she will be a great pilot."

Toni is tall, dark and handsome. He has black hair and a mustache. I detect a tinge of shyness about him. Carol reaches to shake my hand. She is a blond haired woman with a ponytail and a smile as broad as the Mississippi. Toni says, "We own a small private airport in Grove City, Ohio. We charter flights for business trips, hunting trips, fishing trips, you name the place, and I will fly you there. We own a fleet of 14 charter planes.

Our hangar is very large and can accommodate about 50 planes so we also house several privately owned planes of the locals in and around Grove City. My friend, Dave Connelly, handles the mechanics of the planes and keeps them in tip-top condition. Dave has a crew of eight people, all top-notch mechanics."

Toni also gives flying lessons. He will encourage young teens to get interested in flying. "When they become adults, they will know all about an airplane before they even get into one," he says. "I believe people should start young to learn about flying or any other hobby they choose. I teach them all about the airplane and how it functions before they get inside a plane." He says, jokingly of course, "Old Farts, like Uncle Miltie, shouldn't be taking on flying at his age. He could hurt someone." We all had a good laugh at Uncle Miltie's expense.

Two days later I see this gorgeous young man, **Joe Falkner.** He is the expert to end all experts. He boasts, "If it has a moving part, I can fix it, build it, take it apart, or make it into something else. If it doesn't have a moving part, I will make it move. MacGyver could take lessons from me."

I never saw anyone with such a talent for putting things together and making them work. "Sure wish I had you around to work on my car every time it breaks down," I told him. He gives a shy chuckle.

"I own a woodworking shop in Kokomo, Indiana, with my dad. We also have a car repair garage." Joe isn't married. He says, "I am always too busy helping others to seriously look for a wife." There is still hope for him as he is only in his early 30's. I'm thinking...perhaps I can find a nice young lady for him. Joe is part Korean. He is of average height, black hair, and muscular build.

Joe tells us, "My dad met my mother in Korea. They could be married in the service then. Dad was only 18 years old and Mom was 16 and the Chaplain married them at the base in Seoul, Korea. I was born a few months later. I was only 16 when I joined the Army. My parents gave their permission for me to enlist."

Chance says, "I knew he was young, but I never questioned his courage and his sense of duty." He is handsome with a slight oriental look about him. Even though he is only a few years younger than I, I feel like I want to take care of him. He is so sweet.

The day after Joe arrives, **Henry (Hank) Kimball** shows up in his van loaded with munitions. He says, "I have a talent for smelling any and all types of explosives from 10 feet away. My sense of smell is very finely tuned. I have trained myself to recognize the odor of certain chemicals." He will be very beneficial to the project, as we discover later on. Hank says, "I am also proficient with electricity. I can wire your house so well; you will never have to change another light bulb." Hank owns an electrical business in Des Moines, Iowa. He wires homes and businesses for a construction company. He is average height and his coal black hair makes him look very mysterious. He is clean-shaven, but always has a Five-O-Clock shadow. If he ever grows a beard, it will probably cover his whole face and take him all of five hours to grow. He says, "I usually shave twice a day. My wife, Rene, is very grateful that I shave twice a day." Rene was still in Des Moines to keep an eye on the business. Hank says, "We have two children, twin boys. Rene is unable to have any more children. She had a horrible accident when she was helping me wire a house. She fell from a ladder and landed on a metal spike that was protruding from the ground. The spike went through her abdomen, and the doctors had to perform a hysterectomy. Our twins look just like Rene who is tall, dark brown hair, and olive skin. Rene is part French."

Then there is **Billy Harman**. Billy is the weapons expert. Billy says, "You name the weapon and I can tell you what it does, who makes it and how to take it apart." He is also a marksman.

From what the other men are saying, Billy has a gun collection that goes back to before the Civil War. He owns a Gun Shop in Olathe, Kansas, and does very well. Billy has quite an arsenal. He furnishes all the weaponry for our upcoming Raid, and gives us all a refresher course. Billy has a slight build, and the shortest in the group. His beautiful blue eyes smile all the time. They would make Frank Sinatra jealous, and he is as strong as an ox. Billy is an ex-police officer.

The rest of the men are not just along for the ride. They each have a specialty that is like no other.

Ian Murphy is confined to a wheel chair. He says, "I used to fly in Wayne's unit, and on one of my missions I was shot down. Fortunately, I wasn't part of the secret mission that Wayne was on. At least I didn't receive a dishonorable discharge like Wayne. I still think Wayne was railroaded on that deal. I'm lucky enough to collect disability from the government. My wife, **Carmel**, comes along to assist me as my 'gopher'." Ian is an artist. He can do character sketches, portraits, and landscapes; he can draw anything. He is very beneficial to our mission because he is also an expert Cartographer. He tells us, "I work for the State of Nebraska and update their maps every year or so."

He continues, "Carmel and I live on a small acreage in Raymond, Nebraska." He makes the maps from the photos I took when Chance and I flew over the area in Wyoming. He even commented on what a great job I did taking the photos. Chance shows him the photos I took of the complex and he says, "You have captured a lot of detail, which is what I need to make the maps."

"Thanks for saying that, Ian. That sure makes me feel good. I'm really starting to feel like one of the team."

Chapter XIV

THE REST OF THE TEAM

A couple of days go by and the people who have already arrived in town are starting to make their plans with Chance. I keep myself busy at the clinic and Chance fills me in at the end of each day.

Chance asks me to meet him at Putnam & Thurston's on a Wednesday evening and I am introduced to **Mickey Healy,** and his wife, **Terry,** accompanied by Ian and Carmel. Mickey says, "We own a Wheat Farm in Raymond, Nebraska. We have six children and while we are gone, the kids run the farm. We are hunters and climbers." He adds, "Terry and I often meet up with Steve and Joanne and go on climbing adventures in the Rockies." As I meet Mickey and Terry I see that they seem very compatible. They compliment each other in that they are opposites. Mickey is medium height and weight with a great build. He keeps his head shaved, so no one remembers what color his hair is. He is a jolly fellow, mild mannered and always seems happy. Terry is a little more serious in her manner. Mickey was a Medic in the Army, stationed with Chances Unit. Mickey says, "I nursed Ian back to health when he was hospitalized after he was shot down. We became very close friends and have been together ever since."

Ian says, "Mickey saved my life. I didn't give a damn whether I lived or died; I was in such pain I had given up. Mickey kept after me and nagged me so much; I wanted to get better just so I would have the strength to kill him."

We all chuckle. I can feel the love and respect between these two men. We enjoy a very nice meal and I get to know a little about Ian, Carmel, Mickey and Terry. *What devoted people, I thought. They are all different, yet they all seem to be alike.*

Jake and Fran Winters are the next to arrive. _This is a couple who really belong together._ Jake says, "I'm a carpet layer by trade. Fran and I are partners with my brother and his wife in a carpet business in Ann Arbor, Michigan. I was stationed with Chance and his unit but I never actually saw very much combat. I was the Unit Quartermaster, stationed in Vietnam. I can hold my own when it comes to skirmishes. Fran takes care of the books for our company. I'm a freelance carpet layer." Jake says, "My brother and his wife run the company when Fran and I have to travel. We have no children, so there isn't much to tie us down." Jake is small in stature, and Fran is very petite. They do everything together. They are the ultimate partners.

Fran says, "We go dancing every Saturday night and usually enter a dance contest and walk away with first prize." Jake is also a Jack-of-all-trades. Give him a tool and he will show you a hundred ways to use it.

Ken and Freddy Zimmerman are brothers and they enlisted together. Ken says, "We really weren't supposed to do that so we said we were cousins so they wouldn't separate us." They too, do everything together. Ken says, "Once in a while we will have an argument and the fur will fly for a while, but everything gets settled and we go back to acting like nothing happened." Even though they argue and fight a lot you can tell they have a great love for each other. They are sort of comic relief for the rest of the group. They own a gun shop in La Crosse, Wisconsin. Neither of them ever married. Chance says, "No woman will put up with their shenanigans." They don't look at all like brothers, which is why they got away with enlisting as cousins. Ken is burly and tall with dark brown hair, clean-shaven and his beautiful white teeth sparkle when he smiles. Freddie is a lot slimmer than Ken and has reddish blond hair and a goatee. They are about the same height.

Freddie always has a glint in his eyes, as if he is scheming to do something devilish. They are 16 months apart in age.

As everyone seems to be in sync with each other, we meet every night and plan our strategies. I almost feel like a third thumb. They all seem to be so attuned to each other. As the days go by, I am stunned at the way they all accept some of my suggestions. I'm not contributing much; as I depend on the experts do the planning.

Chapter XV

A LITTLE R & R

After a couple of weeks of planning and brushing up on our skills, Carmel, Trudy, Carol, Joanne, Fran, Terry and I go shopping at Filene's Bargain Basement one day. We are mainly looking for clothes for our impending trip. We get a little side tracked and end up at Shearer's Department Store, in their exclusive Women's Department. We buy a few garbs for "going out to dinner and dancing". We approach the men and inform them that we want to go to dinner at a great restaurant and dancing afterwards. After seeing our beautiful evening dresses the men decide to take us up on our suggestion and take their sweethearts out for a night on the town in Boston.

The men are all eyes as we ladies walk into the room at my condo, all decked out in our finery. "Let's go dancing, boys", I say.

Chance says, "Who ever thought of this idea, thank you very much. You ladies look awesome." The rest of the men applaud as we ladies each take a bow and show off our exquisite apparel.

"Ladies," I say, as I clap my hands and the ladies join in, "Let's give the men a big hand too. Don't they look sensational?"

The men all have suits and ties on. Their hair is combed and their faces are shaved or trimmed.

I add, "Wow, you guys smell nice too."

"This will be a night to remember," Chance says.

We women are decked out in our finery and the men are beaming with pride. We act like we are out on our first dates for prom night. We ladies giggle and the men strut as we saunter down the streets of Boston.

Trudy has a darling figure. She wears a soft pink number with a hand knit, soft pink, shawl.

Joanne is tall and slender and wears a Black almost skin tight, dress. She looks gorgeous. She walks like a model.

Carol has a tailored style. She has on a gray pantsuit, which has metallic threads in it. She is stunning with her slim figure and her long legs.

Carmel is part Spanish. She has black shinny hair. She is small and petite. She picked out a red dress, cut low in back that fits very snug to her amazing figure; and about knocks the guy's eyes right out of their heads.

Fran selects a frilly little number. There are about four layers of pastel ruffles on the bottom around the hem. The hemline is at her knees. The dress is pale blue and skintight and she looks absolutely adorable in it. It is a perfect dress for dancing.

Terry found a lovely lilac silk dress with a trumpet skirt. She looks absolutely spectacular. For a person who has had six kids, you wouldn't know it by the looks of her figure.

I wear a black halter dress that I accent with a gold lame shawl and Chance said, "You look extremely sexy tonight Laura." I think I was blushing at that remark.

The men help Ian up and down curbs; otherwise he is pretty proficient with his electric wheel chair. We certainly take Boston by storm that night.

Chance made reservations for us at Boston's most exclusive restaurant, Anthony's Pier 6, on the waterfront. The Doorman, looking like Ahab, greets the customers wearing a bright yellow slicker, with peg leg and all. Spero Panos recommended this restaurant as the highest gross sales in the United States. Spero is friends with the owner, Anthony Anthanas. When Chance called for the reservations he mentioned Spero's name and we are given the best table in the house.

Our table overlooks the Boston Bay where the 'Boston Tea Party' took place. We can watch the 747's landing at Logan Air Port. And what a meal we all have. Everyone has a sample of everything. Anthony comes over to our table and introduces himself. He has trays of food sent to the table that have every combination they serve. We are treated like royalty. We have a great time sampling the delicious cuisine. We talk, laugh and eat for two hours.

Later we find a nightclub where we can dance. On our way back to Worcester we stop at The Meadows, in Framingham. Vaughan Monroe formerly owned the Meadows. The Tex Benneke band is playing this night. Everyone on the dance floor stops dancing and just stands and stares at Jake and Fran as they enter the dance floor and dazzle them with their footwork.

Fran picked the perfect dress for dancing. I say, "I think she bought that dress especially for this occasion."

The two of them are truly amazing together. The band is playing "One O'clock Jump". They have the entire floor to themselves; and what a performance they put on for everyone. They remind me of a music box I had as a child. It had a figure of a man and woman on the top and they danced around and around to the music. Along with the excellent food, Jake and Fran are the highlight of the evening. We can see why they won all those dance contests. When the band ended the fast dance they immediately went into a rumba. Jake and Fran stepped into the transformation as though they were cued. They sure were a couple of crowd pleasers. The band was disappointed when the evening ended, as were all the other people on the dance floor.

When Chance and I return to my condo, we fall onto the couch and sit and savor the evening we just enjoyed. "I don't think I have ever had a more wonderful evening in my entire life," I declare.

"I know I haven't," Chance answers. "On a scale from one to ten, it was definitely a 15."

"Absolutely, and we definitely will have to repeat that experience again very soon.

"You've got a date."

Chapter XVI

TENSE MOMENTS

I have a feeling that Cora is watching me more closely than usual. "What's with you today," I bark, "I'm on your side, remember?"

Cora looks at me with surprise in her eyes. "Why did you say that?"

"You seemed to be questioning my motives for rejecting that last embryo. "The girl has **A.I.D.S.**, for crying out loud. I was instructed to screen each and every fetus for any and all diseases. After taking the girl's history, I was suspicious that she may have A.I.D.S. along with a few other things. She's a druggy and a slut. I ran a few tests and sure enough, I was right."

"Sorry, but I wasn't questioning your motive," Cora comes back. "I was just wondering why you rejected that particular embryo. Now I know."

"I'm sorry Cora. I guess I'm just a little edgy today. Please forgive me for barking at you."

"It's already forgotten," Cora says with a wink.

I had been counseling this girl to seek treatment. Later, I urge her to go to County Hospital and they will see that she receives the proper care. I start her on the 'Cocktail'. I try to get her to clean up her act and cease her present way of life.

I tell Cora, "She tells me she is 15 years old and she ran away from home to get away from her stepfather, who was sexually abusing her. She said she told her mother about it but she didn't believe her. She said she met this really nice guy in the Park and he gave her a place to stay. The next thing she knew she was addicted to drugs and walking the streets for 'tricks'. She told me her Pimp dropped her off at the clinic when he found out she was pregnant."

I check up on her several times at County. They put her in Re-hab, and the last time I checked, the girl was doing fine.

I also find out that she lied about everything. She is 17 years old and is bragging to someone in re-hab about being with 276 men in the past two years. She also brags about keeping a diary and has the names of all the men she slept with. I have led a somewhat naïve and sheltered life and this information, coming from a 17 year old, has a profound impact on me.

Her name is Sharon. We don't use last names at the clinic. She is medium height, dishwater blond hair and a mousy little face. She brags about how she made up a big lie to get sympathy from the abortion clinic doctors. Sharon tells this other person she didn't know who her father is and that her mother was in prison on a drug charge. She has been in a few foster homes, and ran away from most of them.

She tells about one foster parent who had molested her when she was seven years old. She was more or less living on the streets and had been since she was 15. Her personal hygiene left one to believe she had a very low self-esteem.

County Hospital is alerted to the diary and they confiscate it and contact as many of the names as they can. The ones who are contacted all come in to be tested for A.I.D.S. A lot of the names in her journal were fake names. I don't know why anyone would give his real name to a prostitute anyway. I pray that Sharon can get her life turned around. The rate she is going now, she will never see 25.

There isn't much hope for a person with A.I.D.S., however, with the new drugs coming out all the time, they can sure slow down the disease, and the infected person can live a longer life, so long as the drugs are effective for them; and so long as they keep taking their meds. Research is being done all the time to find a cure for the disease. They are very close to developing a vaccine for A.I.D.S.

These are the women I don't mind doing abortions on, even though it goes against the grain for me. They not only don't deserve to become a parent, the child doesn't deserve to be brought into this world with three strikes against it. Besides, I have enough problems deciding how to handle the normal fetuses.

I have to convince Cora that I'm on her side, because if she isn't convinced then we are in big trouble. Usually when a pregnant girl has an abortion, the embryo is killed before it is aborted. Because of what we were instructed to do, we have to see that the fetuses are kept alive. I perfected a method to abort the pregnancy without killing the embryo. This is the procedure that was so repugnant to me when Charles suggested it a few years ago. I say to myself, "I guess now, I'm the Frankenstein," as a shiver runs up my spine. Sometimes the fetuses are farther along than the patient thinks or it will be deformed or under developed. Those are no-brainers.

Charles specifies that he wants the embryos to be no more than six weeks in development. I'm purposely terminating the life of some of the embryos, to slow down the project and give us time to work out our plans. If we send them too many fetuses, it just means more trouble for us. I'm hoping Cora does not catch on to my scheme.

So far, the Courier has picked up 14 live fetuses. Chance is getting a little nervous, as he and I think one live fetus is too many. We have a lot to do and time is not on our side at the moment. Winter will soon be approaching and we must complete our task before the snow starts. I am praying that girls will stop coming in for abortions, at least until we can get organized. Trying to coordinate fourteen plus people is not an easy task, but we need each and every one of them for this mission to succeed. I seem to think Chance has done this before because he is so organized in what has to be done.

While I am attending to my job at the clinic, Chance and the others are busy gathering the equipment we will need for the trip to Wyoming. There are maps to be drawn, equipment to be checked and repaired, if needed. Most of the men came with their own vans, but we still need two more for the trip. Chance contacts a local rental and leases two vans.

Billy Harman takes all of us to the Police firing range, a few at a time. He instructs us on how to shoot, clean, take apart and put back together, the gun or guns we will be using. Billy introduces his arsenal to each person and lets us chose which one would best suit our preference. Some of the men, however, own gun shops and have their own favorites that they brought with them. This was actually mainly for us women who didn't know that much about guns. I knew how to shoot, and how to clean a gun, but I didn't actually know that much about the gun itself. I was grateful for the refresher course, as were the rest of the women. Some of the men, even though they were in the Army, needed a refresher course also. It isn't like the old West. We don't carry guns and draw when provoked. I also wanted to get acquainted with the gun I choose.

Some of the weapon choices are: the Winchester 1200 12-gauge shotguns with the plastic pistol grip Choate stock; .357 Magnum lever-action carbines. There are quite a few .45 automatics, which most of us take as a back-up gun. A Rossi Model 92 with its sixteen-inch barrel; There are several .357 Magnum revolvers; some 44 Magnum Desert Eagles; and Beretta 93-R select-fire pistols to choose from. There are also extra

30-round 9 mm magazines and a submachine gun with a hammer feature rather than a 3-round burst. There is plenty of extra ammunition for all the weaponry, for target practice and for real use.

I choose the Beretta 93-R, as do most of the other women, along with a .45 automatic. The Beretta seems easier for a small hand to manage. The .45 is also suggested for us women. We have trouble getting it through our heads that we may have to actually shoot someone, but we understand we will have to protect ourselves and we will shoot if we must.

Chapter XVII

BOMB SCARE

One Wednesday afternoon a phone call comes into the clinic from a concerned citizen about how they overhear a conversation on someone's cell phone. They tell us that our Clinic is going to be bombed. In a situation like this we act first and consider whether it's a hoax later. Immediately, Cora calls the authorities and we are instructed to clear the building. Cora instantly jumps into her military mode and everything runs smoothly. We try to be discreet, so the would-be bomber won't be tipped off just in case they are watching the building and we do not want to alarm the patients. We have six patients in the clinic at this time.

Some are ushered out the front door and some out the side door. The side door goes directly into the parking lot. We tell them one of the doctors has an emergency at home and he needs our help and we will be closing the clinic for the rest of the day.

They are instructed to get into their cars and go home and we will resume the interviews and examinations tomorrow. No one wants any of the patients exposed to the press. We know that the minute the police are called, the press will get wind of it and all hell will break loose. These kids are having enough trouble trying to decide whether to have an abortion or not; they don't need their faces in the newspaper or on the six o'clock news.

No sooner do we get everyone out, the police arrive. They also take precautions, and arrive in unmarked cars. There is a time frame of about 45 minutes from when the call comes in to when the bombers are supposed to show.

The caller said they had mentioned a time, which gives us about 15 more minutes to get ourselves away from the situation. We are instructed to leave some of the cars in the parking lot. If the perpetrators see no cars, they might get suspicious and leave. Because we are the only ones left, Cora, Mary Jean, two of the nurses and I go across the street for safety. We just get settled inside the neighborhood grocery and a man and woman try to get in the back door of the clinic. The police are already in place to nab those idiots.

There are several buildings surrounding the clinic and the S.W.A.T. team is waiting for them. When the Police nab them, they find dynamite in a 'Doctor's bag'. These two are well known for their repugnance of abortion Doctors. They are a husband and wife team, Harry and Clara Thurmond; self-proclaimed abortion police.

They are charged with conspiring to commit bodily harm and attempted murder. From all reports, they are still in prison today. I make an executive decision and close the clinic for the rest of the day and we five ladies go out for a drink to calm our nerves. I would have preferred the hoax.

The press shows up, but it is all over and everyone manages to duck out before they have to answer any questions. We leave the grocery store like we have nothing to do with what is going on across the street.

When I tell Chance about our afternoon of excitement, he is furious. He says, "Thank God you were all alerted, and you got out of there." I didn't tell him how frightened we all were, but I didn't have to, he knew. As he hugged me, he could feel my trembling body.

"God bless that good Samaritan who called to warn us," I added. "I shudder to think what would have happened, if we hadn't been forewarned."

Chance says, "Things really have to change in this country. People just can't go around threatening other people like that. The government never should have legalized abortion."

I said, "I know, it is a horrible way to deal with an unwanted pregnancy. What ever happened to having the baby and giving it up for adoption if the person doesn't want to keep the baby? There are plenty of married people out there who find they can't have children and would love to adopt one. The Government makes it too hard for people to adopt children, and too easy to have an abortion."

Chapter XVIII

ROMANCE

Chance's team is so good at what they do, Chance is worrying for nothing. He is lucky to have such good and loyal friends. Not too many people can make that statement. I am honored to be included in this group; and include me, they do. Unaware of what is going on behind my back, I am in for a big surprise.

There are several wooded areas in and around Worcester. The men scout around and find the perfect spot in the Northwest section of the Worcester area for my initiation ceremony into their group. The area, at that particular time, is under-developed. There has been a lot of building of homes in that area since. Our 'private' woods have escaped development so far. The spot that is selected for the ceremony is right in the middle of the wooded area. There is a small clearing surrounded by tall trees and a lot of shrubbery. We can tell wild animals live in these woods because of the markings they leave behind. We try not to disturb too much of the underbrush because we don't want the wild animals to go away. There is a mashed down grassy area where it looks like deer might have made their bed.

The wives assemble a feast of wine and fresh fruit and the men set up the rest. It's a good thing it is an isolated spot; for if we were seen one might think we are some sort of cult or worse, devil worshipers. No one is too sure who actually came up with the ceremony, but it is beautiful.

All the wives had to go through the same ceremony. Even though Chance and I are not husband and wife, I am so special to them that they make an exception in my case. A crown of flowers is made for my hair and a special wine is served. The men made up the ceremony when they decided to bring their wives into their confidence. Each one of the men shakes my hand and welcomes me into the group. The women follow suit. *I'm wondering why all the fuss, we seem to all get along so well, I didn't know why they had to go through so much formality.*

Later that night, when all is quiet and everyone has gone to their assigned Motels and we are alone in my condo, Chance seizes the moment, takes me by the hand and says, "Laura, my love, will you do me the honor of becoming my wife?"

For the first time in my life, I am speechless. My pause brings a look on Chance's face as if to say, *"Oh no, what have I done? She probably thinks I'm nuts."*

The look vanishes when I say, "I would be honored to be your wife, Chance." "I only hope you aren't just caught up in the moment and will hate yourself in the morning." I say, breathlessly.

"Fat chance of that happening, my lady. I have loved you since the first moment I laid eyes on you," he confesses. "Why do you think I am no longer with Alma?" "She just couldn't measure up to you."

The only reply I can utter is, "Thanks Alma."

He takes me in his arms and kisses me. It is the most passionate kiss I have ever had. With a Shakespearean flare he says, "My lady, I love you with all my heart and all my breath. I am so glad you said yes. If you had said no, I would have been forced to do myself in."

"I'm sure glad I won't have that on my conscience. I would hate to be the cause of your demise. And I love you too," I reply. He holds me in his strong arms and kisses me again and again. We seem to melt into each other's arms. He picks me up and carries me into the bedroom... (**FADE TO BLACK**)

Chapter XIX

I DO

The following week a Justice of the Peace in Auburn, Mass. marries us. We want to keep everything low key and a secret, at least until all this is over. It is a very simple ceremony. The men and their wives stand up for us. I wear a beautiful off white suit. I have a simple bouquet of yellow daisies.

I am a little sad that I can't tell Mary Jean and Cora about the wedding. I would have loved to have them stand up for me. As it turns out, I had a plethora of people standing up for me. The entire group joined us.

After the wedding ceremony, we all go to Putman & Thurston's for a wonderful dinner. Spero Panos is there and when he learns we were just married, he has the chef prepare a beautiful Wedding Cake for us and it is presented at the end of the meal.

Spero informs us, "In the restaurant business we always have cakes on hand. They are made in advance and frozen; they are then defrosted and decorated for different occasions when needed." Chance and I are overcome by the friendly, warm gesture that Spero has shown us. I stand up, throw my arms around Spero, and give him a big kiss on his cheek. He blushes and says, "Well, thank you very much." It is the perfect ending to a perfect day.

I have a hard time explaining what a wonderful feeling it is to have so many amazing friends. "I feel euphoric," I tell everyone.

I hadn't realized that I had fallen in love with Chance until he proposed. I have always admired him greatly. I'm in awe of his courage and leadership. I really didn't know what love was all about until this man stood before me and poured his heart out to me. As he speaks, I too am filled with these same feelings and didn't even realize it. I wasn't able to understand why

I would tingle all over whenever he came too close or touched my hand. There has been just too much heavy stuff going on these past few months to give my feelings any validity. *"That split-second vision that I had of the two of us together, wasn't just so much fantasy after all,"* I think to myself.

For the sake of the project we are keeping our separate living quarters. We will take turns spending time together at each others place, but we make sure we spend the nights alone. It wouldn't have mattered much to anyone if they knew we were married, but we just couldn't take the likelihood that our relationship might jeopardize what we have to do.

Chance and I both agree that this project will be our priority until it is finished. All the others agreed that this is too important to make a mistake now. There is never a time that we think we **cannot** pull this off. The men and their wives are behind the undertaking to the bitter end.

I soon learn what really has brought this group of men and their wives together. Chance has a few things up his sleeve that I don't know about.

He seems very nervous about this secret he is keeping from me; but he dares not say anything just yet. I sense something is amiss but I never, in my wildest dreams, ever thought that the relationship with these men is as strong as I find out later. . .

Chapter XX

THE GAB SESSION

 The wheels have been set in motion and we are ready for our big raid to take place. Chance receives more instructions from Dr. Charles Knight. Three months have passed since we started the project, and we estimate that about 45 fetuses have been taken to the facility in the mountains from all the Abortion Clinics. I presume Charles instructed the other clinics on how to abort the fetus and keep it alive.
 Chance says, "I have been picking Charles' brain and I figured out that he has about four other clinics from which he is receiving the fetuses, besides this one. These fetuses come from all around the country. I don't know just how long the "geniuses" with Charles have been working on their scheme, but I estimate it to be at least three years. From the looks of the facility we saw from the air, it would have taken at least that long to develop what they have there."
 Chance adds, "We have to work fast if we are going to close them down before they can go any farther with their experiments. You see, what they are doing, in their own narcissistic way, is trying to make their own private **"Perfect Society"**. They have developed a way to maintain the aborted fetuses and bring them to maturity. They do genetic altering on the fetuses so that their DNA is not matched to any other human being, other than each other. They actually turn all the fetuses into siblings."
 Chance and I never did figure out why they did that. He spoke to several of the scientists but apparently they have been sworn to secrecy, or perhaps they, too, don't really know why or what they are doing, as they clam up about any and all of their experiments.

Chance says, "I think perhaps Charles is the only one who knows the complete details of the entire project. He would be just the type to keep everything locked away in his own mind. He wouldn't want too many of his colleagues knowing what he's up to. The other scientists have been assigned each to their own project. No one seems to know what the other is working on. The plan is to bring the fetuses to maturity and then turn them into mechanical beings so that by the time they are adults they will be controlled to do anything they are told to do, without question."

I add, "They feed them the "perfect nutrition". They teach them to think alike; and teach them their version of history and instruct them on what to do for the future, to create "New World Order". Sound familiar? Hitler all over again, the "Master Race", only this time they are taking it to new heights. They aren't going to be satisfied with just starting a perfect society, they also plan to eliminate what we know as "Our World". Is that about right, Chance?"

"I'm afraid so Laura."

Chance and I are having dinner at my place with the other men and their wives. Chance starts on a tirade about the government and what is wrong with this country. He says, "First of all a toxic chemical has been introduced into our food and diet soda. It is a sugar substitute. A prominent chemical company has developed the product and the government knows that it is poison to our system. However, the government is in 'bed' with this chemical company and they have ignored the warnings of its deadly side effects."

"And, of course," I add, "We all know, the government always sides with the **BIG** money."

Several of the men are nodding their heads and agreeing with me. Chance continues, "This chemical is not only in diet soda, but it is in over 5000 other products that are consumed by the public, including children's vitamins and some non-diet gum. What the public doesn't know is this sugar substitute makes a person crave sweets and increases their appetite, so they eat more. So, if the consumer really wants to lose weight, they should **not** drink 'diet soda'. This sugar substitute turns into formaldehyde when it reaches a temperature of 80 degrees. What is our body's normal temperature?"

"98.6 degrees," I contribute. "I know that was a rhetorical question, but I just couldn't help myself." Everyone starts to chuckle.

"BINGO!!" Chance says. "Think about how hot the large trucks get, in the summer months that deliver the diet soda to the stores."

Uncle Miltie adds, "Hey, during the summer months these trucks become extremely hot. I guess I never gave it much thought, Chauncey, but when you stop to think about it, this could kill off a tremendous amount of people eventually."

"That's exactly right! I think they are getting scared because people are starting to live longer." Chance says, "Government agencies are also allowing deadly chemicals to seep into our drinking water and into our food supply through hog farms, pesticides, and non organic fertilizers," Chance continues. "Unless the consumer starts growing his or her own food, we could be slowly poisoning ourselves with what we buy in the super markets. Not to mention the new radiation method they want to put our food through." Chance pauses and says, "I wonder what genius thought of that? Someone sure sold the government a bill of goods. And don't even get me started about **Fluoride**. It's a by product of aluminum and the government didn't know what to do with it, so they decided to put it in toothpaste. Aluminum is one of the causes of Alzheimer's."

Trudy says, with a slight grin, "One of these days we might all be glowing in the dark."

"And all of this is in the name of science." Hank interjects.

I ask, "Do any of you ever wonder where all these new diseases come from? It seems like we have a new crop of them every 10 or 20 years. When one gets cured, another shows up. As a doctor, I often wonder about this. Leprosy is one disease that has reared its ugly head again, since all the 'boat people' from Haiti came here. They brought this disease with them, and the government is keeping it under wraps. There is no cure for this strain of leprosy. Just like there is no cure for the new strain of tuberculoses that has also reared its ugly head."

Hank says, "You know, I hate to say this but, we should close our borders until these deadly diseases can be gotten under control. A.I.D.S. is running rampant in Africa and Asia. If we keep letting these people into our country, we are going to have a gigantic problem; even worse than we have already. Who knows what diseases are coming over our borders from the South?"

Chance says, "Closing our boarders would be a drastic measure, Hank, but I think you are right. We do need to start getting serious about the foreign element bringing all their diseases into our country. Not to mention the fact that most of them are illegally here. Perhaps better screening for certain diseases should be considered. Perhaps there should be a place where they can be quarantined before they are allowed to enter society. There are a lot of possibilities to be considered. And we also need to screen people better because there are a lot of terrorists who are coming in under the radar."

Hank pipes up and adds, "Absolutely, just what are those people thinking, anyway?"

Billy adds, "The EPA claims to be concerned with the environment, but in reality, they're the ones who are destroying it. Actually, there's nothing wrong with the environment; if they leave nature alone, Mother Nature will correct it herself. She has been doing that since the beginning of time."

After further discussing the horrors of what these scientists are doing, I add, "Their time would have been best spent finding cures for all these new diseases, instead of wasting their time with aborted fetuses and trying to perfect a flawed human society."

"This may sound silly but imagine what would have happened if "Man" had been around during the dinosaur age, and started a campaign to 'Save the Dinosaur'. That would have been one big mess. No one needs to save the owls, or some fish in a pond, or some tree that is about to be eliminated," Willie says. He continues, "You're right, Billy, Nature has been taking care of herself for millions of years, and she will continue to do so long after **humans** are extinct. Do you know that there is a tree in California that is **causing** "Air Pollution? "Why don't the EPA people get on top of that one? Get rid of it. Why do we need it?"

Carman adds, "I read something about that Willie, but I thought someone was just pulling my leg."

Chance says, "Our government originally was set up to never interfere with or attempt to control our lives and our property, EVER! Government's basic function is to protect the citizens from criminals and protect our God given rights to life, liberty, property and our individual pursuit of happiness. We, as individuals can also perform this function i.e. 'The right to bear arms'. Our freedom means freedom from governmental interference in the economic life of the people. Read your Constitution and the Declaration of Independence."

"The founders of this country fought against a Socialistic government. The signers of the Declaration of Independence were hunted down by the Red Coats and murdered. Let's not spit in the faces of the founders of this great land by allowing Socialism to take over our lives."

Chance adds, "There are big money people in this country, and world, who are manipulating bureaucrats and federal officials to do their bidding. Usually all it takes is an envelope full of money. If these people ever find out about us, they will have us all eliminated. All you need to do is look at the list of foreign contributors to some of our politician's campaigns. Most of them, however, hide the names of the contributors and the countries where they live. Oh, by the way, just for the record, there is no such thing as "Global Warming". It's Climate Change; it has been happening since the beginning of time. That's another ploy to get the "Tribunal" together for "New World Order". It's so politicians have something to talk about to divert our attention away from the real problems."

Chance says, "George Washington said it best, 'Government is not reason. It is not eloquence. It is force. Like fire, it is a dangerous servant and a fearful master.' He understood very clearly that government is dangerous. Our founders also realized that rights do not come from government – rights come from God. This is the principle of Americanism. Government is only there to protect our God given rights. Government does not grant rights to people – People grant rights to government. We are a Republic – we were never meant to be a Democracy."

"In a Democracy, majority rules, which means, that there are going to be some people who will be losing their rights and freedoms. As real Americans, we must stop Socialism in our country, and return to what our founding fathers fought for and lost their lives for; and that is, our God given right to freedom – freedom from the government."

"George Washington believed that politicians, who push Socialism in this country, are guilty of Treason. Most politicians of today are guilty of Treason. Think about that!"

Chance had done a lot of research on his own; way before I came into the picture, and he discovered that the poisons and diseases that are being introduced into our towns and cities are being done very selectively. Chance tells us, "They are picking and choosing in which cities to eliminate the population, and which cities to leave alone. For instance, "Podunk, USA", is no threat to them, but New York, Los Angeles, Chicago etc., are a big threat and the easiest to eliminate. Everyone, of course, is puzzled at why the drug dealers can't be stopped." Chance continues, "I know that certain federal agencies don't want the drugs to stop flowing into this country. That way they have better control over the masses by filling them with mind altering drugs. Just look at all the children who get rambunctious in school, the teachers immediately want to put those children on a drug so they won't have to deal with them. I also put parents in this same category; they don't want to deal with their children so they have the doctor prescribe a drug so they can keep them 'calm'. And now those drugged up kids are going on shooting sprees in schools and movie theaters because the drugs have made them go nuts. Parents need to start raising their own kids and not the government or the drug companies."

Miltie says, "Parents and children need to get off all the drugs. The drug companies shouldn't be allowed to advertise on TV. If a person is caught selling drugs on the street, he is thrown in jail, but the drug companies get away with it. Have you ever listened to the side effects on some of those drugs they are pushing? ("May cause death.") Sure doesn't make me want to take them. I have never encouraged anyone to take prescription drugs without first talking about a natural alternative."

Chip contributes, "It is easier to lead **zombies** around by the nose than it is people in their right minds. After all, look what happened to the American Indians. They were so whacked on locoweed or mescaline (i.e. smoking the peace pipe) that they gave their country away; and look what we have allowed the politicos to do to it. Now they are legalizing marijuana in some states. Don't they know about oils? Good grade oils do more for people than marijuana could ever do and you wouldn't have a bad drug in your system."

Chance nods and says, "They are putting video surveillance cameras on street corners in "high crime" areas, in the guise of cutting down on crime, or for use as traffic control. What they are really doing is keeping tabs on all of us. If this keeps up we won't be able to leave our homes without permission from "Big Brother"."

I comment, "They have surveillance cameras in banks to catch bank robbers on tape. They are putting cameras at intersections in the guise of catching people who go through red lights. Who do they think they are dealing with? Do they think we are all ignorant? I don't know how they can see anything on those tapes anyway. Are they actually able to identify anyone from those tapes?"

Chance says with a chuckle, "Well, true, Laura, but my point goes a little deeper than that. Some criminals are so well known they know who these people are just by their body language. My biggest objection is if we allow these surveillance cameras to be put in high crime neighborhoods, and at intersection, the next thing you know they will be putting these cameras in your neighborhoods and mine." Chance adds, "Every time you leave your home, "Big Brother" will be watching. How much privacy do you think you will have then?"

"I know for a fact that a lot of the big Malls around the country have already put surveillance cameras in the common areas," adds Joe.

"What is it going to take before people stop letting the "bleeding hearts" ruin our country? We don't need "Big Daddy" monitoring our every move. We cannot allow anyone to take away our freedom of privacy. If the Legislators would stop making laws that protect the criminals, there wouldn't be as much crime as we have today," Chance continues. "Law abiding citizens have the right to protect themselves against a person who is bent upon doing them harm. A person who commits a crime against society should not be allowed to live among innocent, law-abiding people.

A child molester should never be allowed to enter society after he or she has been convicted of that crime. Pedophilia **cannot** be cured, yet the judges in this Country either set them free or slap a very light sentence on them; and they are out on the streets molesting and or murdering more children." Chance adds. "Chemical castration does not work. Unless they are going to keep a pedophile in a confined area and administer the chemical to him, there is no way he will take it on his own. The Pedophiles like what they do to children."

I agree and say, "The courts and prisons keep releasing these thugs on society and they wonder why we have so much crime in this country. Instead of concentrating on who has or doesn't have guns, they should be concentrating on how the **criminals** are getting guns."

"You are absolutely right, Laura," Chance says. He continues with his rage, "Inanimate objects don't commit crimes...crimes are committed by people who use those objects. Whether it is guns or knives, when a person makes a choice to use these items to commit a crime it isn't the item that commits the crime...it's the person who chooses to use the item."

I interject, "I think Einstein once said, "The definition of insanity is doing the same thing over and over and expecting different results."

"Yes, Einstein did say that and it sure makes sense to me. If you can't learn after the first time that something isn't going to work, try something else. Too bad our Politicians can't learn that. They seem to repeat the same old stuff year after year and expect different results."

Miltie says, "I just wish people would start to realize just what is going on in their neighborhoods and start objecting to all this ridiculous nonsense."

Hank says, "Same goes for illegal drugs and alcohol, Chauncey."

"Absolutely, Hank, People blame alcohol when they get behind the wheel of a car and kill someone. The person who chooses to take a drink, and another, and another, is the one responsible for getting behind the wheel of an automobile and killing someone. The alcohol isn't responsible. . .the person is."

Willie says, "Well, kids see the pro-athletes and movie stars using drugs and alcohol and getting away with their bad behavior, so it stands to reason they are going to try it themselves. I think they should ban a pro-athlete from playing sports for life if he is caught using drugs or committing a crime while under the influence. The same goes for a Movie Star. Once they are convicted of using or dealing drugs, they should be ousted from the Movie industry. Instead they make heroes out of them. What do you suppose goes through a child's mind when they see all this? Morality needs to come back in this country."

Uncle Miltie joins in with, "Now we have to put up with "hate crimes". I never heard of anything so utterly ridiculous. When a person does harm to another person whether it's a beating or killing, isn't that out of hate? I never saw anyone get killed out of like. Why does everything have to have a label? So far as I know, all crime comes from hate. All of a sudden some "bleeding heart" comes up with a new buzz word, 'It's a hate crime'. Now we have to make new laws to include a "hate crime". When did this Country become so stupid?" Milton continues, "They talk about the "Dumbing-down of America". This is really the dumbest."

Chance says, "'Dumbing down' isn't our only problem, albeit a big one, another problem with the government is the way they raise taxes so high that both parents are forced to go to work just to make ends meet. When taxes were introduced into this country, around 1913, only .03% of the workers earnings were to be deducted for taxes. However, when the politicians saw how great it was to spend all this money that was pouring in, they decided to increase the tax. They not only increased the income tax, they put a sales tax on all items sold to the consumer. Then the States jumped on the bandwagon and decided to add a few more taxes on the consumer through property tax, sales tax, inheritance tax and user tax. If this isn't double and triple dipping, I don't know what is. If they would just put an end to Welfare alone we wouldn't be paying so much in taxes."

Chance continues. "They raised our income taxes year after year so they can support all their 'special interests', until wage earners are now handing over almost 65% of their wages to the government. That includes sales tax, user tax, State tax, city tax, property tax etc. And this tax burden is on only a small percentage of people who actually own homes and have a job. The rest are on the dole. Everyone needs to understand that **WE** are the government and **WE** don't need 'Big Daddy' telling us what is good for us. We know what is good for us and what is bad for us. As a country, America needs law and order; but not to the point where a law abiding citizen forfeits the right to freedom, privacy, and happiness."

Chance pulls a piece of paper out of his back pocket. He holds it up and says, "Here is an article that appeared in a small town news paper. I love what this guy has to say. Let me read it to you.

What has America become?

"Has America become the land of the special interest and home of the double standard? Let's see: if we lie to the congress, it's a felony and if the congress lies to us it's just politics; if we dislike a black person, we're racist and if a black dislikes whites, it's their 1st Amendment right; the government spends millions to rehabilitate criminals and they do almost nothing for the victims; in public schools you can teach that homosexuality is OK, but you better not use the word God in the process; you can kill an unborn child, but it's wrong to execute a mass murderer; we don't burn books in America, we now rewrite them; we got rid of the communist and socialist threat by renaming them Progressives; we are unable to close our border with Mexico but have no problem protecting the 38th parallel in Korea; if you protest against the Presidents policies you're a terrorist, but if you burned an American flag or George Bush in effigy it was your 1st Amendment right. You can have pornography on TV or the internet, but you better not put a nativity scene in a public park during Christmas; we have eliminated all criminals in America, they are now called sick people; we can use a human fetus for medical research, but it's wrong to use an animal.

We take money from those who work hard for it and give it to those who don's want to work; we all support the Constitution, but only when it supports our political ideology; we still have freedom of speech, but only if we are being politically correct; parenting has been replaced with Ritalin and video games; the land of opportunity is now the land of hand outs; the similarity between Hurricane Katrina and the gulf oil spill is that neither president did anything to help.

And how do we handle a major crisis today? The government appoints a committee to determine who's at fault, then threatens us, passes a law, raises our taxes, tells us the problem is solved so they can get back to their reelection campaign. **What has happened to the land of the free and home of the brave?** -Ken Huber, Tawas City."

Chance says, "How about that for an editorial?

Willie puts in his two cents on the subject by adding, "We certainly don't need the government telling us how to spend **our** money. But we sure need to tell the government how to spend **our** money. They have made the citizens of this country so used to the handouts that most of them don't know how to survive without them."

"I think I speak for everyone here in saying, we agree with you 100 percent, Chauncey, and you too Willie," Hank says. "The more money the government obtains the more money the government will spend. One of these days, if we aren't careful, we will be working solely for the government and have to depend on them for food, clothing, medical and everything else for which we now depend solely on ourselves. "Everyone should know what that is; it's called **"COMMUNISM" or "SOCIALISM". Look out folks! It's coming!** If a person tells you he is a Progressive Democrat, he is telling you he is a Communist. That's the new word for Communism.

Several of the people in the room say, "That's a great article. Thanks for reading it to us".

I concur. "We don't need Socialized Medicine in this country. And we certainly don't need a Communist government. It has already been proven that Communism does not work".

"You've got that right, Laura," Chance says, "Canada has Socialized Medicine and it isn't working for them. Sometimes a patient has to wait three to six months before they can have an operation that they desperately need. Some people have even waited as long as a year for their much-needed operation. I read of several people who didn't make it. They died waiting." Chance gets up and starts to pace around the room with his hands waving in the air. "This cannot be stressed enough; **"New World Order"** is another name for **COMMUNISM**. It is even printed on our one-dollar bill, "Novus Ordo Seclorium", translation.... "New Order of Ages".

I am surprised about that and say, "Really? That's very interesting, Chance; I never gave it much thought."

Everyone takes out some bills from their pocket and they begin to examine them. Tom asks, "What does this eye on a pyramid stand for? I used to know, but haven't thought about it in years."

"The First Continental Congress requested Benjamin Franklin and a group of men to come up with a Seal. It took them four years to accomplish this task and another two years to get it approved." Chance says. As everyone is looking at their dollar bills, Chance continues, "Notice the face is lighted and the western side is dark. This country was just beginning. We had not begun to explore the West or even decided what we could do for Western Civilization. The pyramid is uncapped signifying that we were not even close to being finished. Inside the capstone you have the all 'Seeing Eye', an ancient symbol for divinity. It was Franklin's belief that one man could not do it alone, but a group of men, with the help of God, could do anything. The Latin above the pyramid, ANNUIT COEPTIS, means God has favored our undertaking."

Uncle Miltie says, "That is very interesting. I don't think we ever learned that in school. What about the United Nations, Chauncey? People should be very aware that the U.N. is the tip of the ice berg when it comes to 'New World Order'."

Chance says, "You're right, Milton, the U.N. is very dangerous to this country. One of our service men refused to wear the U.N. uniform. He knew what he was doing by changing his "colors", so to speak. The Army tried to court martial him or some sort of discipline like that. I'm not too sure what happened to him. The press, more or less, let it drop."

"Or perhaps the Press was told to let it drop," Miltie adds. Everyone nods. "And speaking of the press, has anyone noticed how the Media seems to be running everything. They seem to decide elections, who should be doing this and who should be doing that. What's that all about?"

Chance continues, "Not only the Media seems to be getting away with the proverbial murder; but more and more Americans are coming to the realization that the United States membership in the United Nations poses a very real threat to our survival as a free and independent nation. Another thing we must keep in mind is that the U.N.'s basic philosophy is anti-American and pro-totalitarian. Our Declaration of Independence proclaims the "self-evident" truth that "men...are endowed by their Creator with certain unalienable rights." But, in its Covenant of Civil and Political Rights; the U.N. ignores God's existence, implies that **it** grants rights, and then repeatedly claims power "as provided by law" to cancel them out of existence. If any government can place restrictions on such fundamental rights as freedom of speech, the right to keep and bear arms, freedom of the press, association, movement and religion, soon there will be no such freedoms. We need to start electing Statesmen instead of Career Politicians."

Tom says, "I live by the fact that we do indeed have rights. The second Amendment states, "A well regulated Militia, being necessary to the security of a Free State, the right of the people to keep and bear Arms, **shall not be infringed**." I have always thought people conveniently misinterpret the second Amendment. I think it speaks for itself."

Chance says, "You are correct on that Tom. Another Amendment that is misinterpreted is the first Amendment; which reads, "Congress shall make no law respecting an establishment of religion, or prohibiting the free exercise thereof; or abridging the freedom of speech, or of the press...etc." It says nothing about the separation from Church and State. It merely states that the government cannot interfere with religion. But the **Atheists** and the **ACLU** have to step in and make a big stink about displaying a decorated Christmas tree on government property. There is nothing in our Constitution that says the government can't display a Christmas tree on government property. For some reason, these Atheists seem to get away with their misguided interpretation of the Constitution."

Chance takes a detour in the conversation and says, "Another thing that really bothers me is, societies children are being raised by strangers who couldn't care less whether they are taught right from wrong. Actually they aren't hired to teach the children anything, they are just high paid baby sitters. Children are getting farther and farther away from their parents influence every day. This is exactly what the government wants to happen. The less influence the parents have the more influence the government will have." Chance adds, "I don't want any of you to think that

I'm against our government or our Country. Don't get me wrong. I love this country. It's the only country I ever want to live in; however, I think we need to look at whom we elect to run our country. Some of these career politicians want the government running every aspect of our lives. That's what I am against. I am against a corrupt government and that seems to be where we are heading right now. I repeat, we need to elect Statesmen to run the country and we need term limits.

Miltie says, "We know exactly what you are saying Chauncey. I agree with you all the way. I'm sick of the government's nose up my pant leg all the time. We do need to elect some Statesmen to go to Washington instead of those career Politicians. Some of them have been in Washington for decades and they still haven't accomplished anything."

I interrupt the conversation to serve cake to everyone. I said, "I hope everyone likes strawberries."

Chance says, "I don't hear any objections from anyone."

I give everyone a piece of cake and Hank is already licking his lips. "Down boy, there is enough for everyone. I made two cakes just to make sure."

"Good thinking, Laura," Chance says.

As I'm handing out the cake I add, "I guess a day care center is a good racket to be in today. These people are making fortunes and the children are becoming the banes of society."

"Absolutely, Laura," Chance says. "Parents don't want to spend, what little time they have with their children, disciplining them, so they compensate by becoming their "buddies". This is a very bad decision to make. Parents were never meant to be buddies to their children," Chance continues. "Now don't start gnashing your teeth," he says, as he looks around the room at the others.

Hank throws his hands in the air and says, "You won't get an argument from me."

"Me either," Uncle Miltie adds.

Freddie adds, "I understand what you are saying, Chance. Our sister's boy, Justin, can get pretty nasty to his parents sometimes."

Kenny says, "That's when I usually step in and straighten him out. He changes his tone real quick when Freddie and I are around."

Chance continues, "Everyone knows there are a lot of good kids out there and they should be proud of their standing. But one must admit that if children don't receive the proper upbringing and good discipline and guidance some of them can and will end up on the wrong side of the law."

"You won't get an argument from me on that point," I add.

"A parent's role is to see that the children grow up with values and are taught right from wrong. Children want and expect parents to give them guidance and discipline," Chance continues. "Somewhere along the line, this task has been transferred to the government and/or the baby sitter. Since the government took over the rearing of our children they have become obnoxious and mouthy. They have no respect for adults, or property, or anything else that gets in their way. It used to be that when Mom or Dad said, "don't", it meant, "DON'T". Now when the parent says don't the kid looks at him or her with a smirk and they do what ever they damn well please. 'BIG DADDY' is watching; and they know that if Mom or Dad lays a hand on them they will go to jail. Of course, the kids think this is great, until it happens, then it is too late to take it back. The damage is done and a family is torn apart forever. Because of a few people who beat their children to death, the government and the 'bleeding hearts' have decided that the rest of the parents don't have the brains to raise their own kids. Punish the **guilty**, leave the **innocent** alone. Parents are also supposed to be role models for their children," Chance continues. "Parents should conduct their lives in such a manner that their children can look up to them and be proud of them. These fragile little lives do not need the government handing out the rules of discipline. These fragile little lives need the parents as their guides. Parents have an obligation to see that their children are nourished, educated and clothed and have a moral upbringing, not an environment that is covered in deceit and misconduct. How can a child take their parents seriously if the parents can't conduct themselves in a moral and respectable manner? Adults have certain privileges that a child does not have and the child needs to be taught those differences."

Uncle Miltie says, "If one more person mentions 'Politically Correct' to me, I will punch them dead in the face. That's just another way of saying 'lie through your teeth'."

Everyone applauds and shouts, "Right on Uncle Miltie."

Chance says, "If anyone is interested, the new policy that most of our schools are adopting, "zero tolerance", is unconstitutional. Think about it for a while..."zero tolerance" is stepping on our freedom of speech, freedom of worship, freedom to bear arms, and the pursuit of happiness. Actually there is no such thing as "zero tolerance". It just doesn't exist. It's just another buzz phrase."

"My God, Chauncey," Milton says, "You're right. I never thought about it that way. But you are right. Why do we let our schools get away with that crap?"

"Good question," Chance says, "Why *are* we letting our schools get away with it?" Chance adds, "Could it be because our schools are run by Bleeding Heart Liberals? If the Left has their way, we would all be working for a Socialist Government."

I add, "Perhaps we should be looking into that aspect before everything gets completely out of hand." I continue, "What about the six year old boy who kissed that little girl on the playground. He was suspended from school for sexual harassment."

"Now if that isn't the epitome of ridiculous, I don't know what is," Bobby Joe adds.

"Good grief, Chauncey, what is this world coming to? How do we stop this madness?" Willie asks.

Chance just shakes his head and looks down at the floor. "I don't know, Willie, but we had better wake up soon or it will be too late. Perhaps if there were more people like us, our problems would be solved."

I say, "Even the day care centers aren't concerned with whether little 'Johnny' and or 'Jane' has a decent meal or decent supervision; but they sure jump when little 'Johnny' kisses one of the other little girls. The Moms and Dads are too busy trying to make ends meet; so little 'Johnny' and or 'Jane" grow up thinking no one cares. The children make their own rules and start shooting at their classmates or teachers and end up in Jail for the rest of their lives, or worse they could be dead. The government will not allow parents to discipline their children anymore and they wonder why they are running amok."

"Now some of the courts want to try 10 and 11 year old children as adults because they killed someone." I am almost in tears, I pause to compose myself and continue. "Those 10 and 11 year olds wouldn't be killing anyone if Mom and Dad were allowed to raise them without interference from the government."

"I agree wholeheartedly," Chance, says, "Children need structure and rules in their lives, and they need it from their parents, not from the government. Without this structure and these rules they will do anything that sounds like fun; whether it is right or wrong. Children don't have the experience and knowledge that adults have. They need that guiding hand of their parents. The government needs to give the child-rearing back to the parents and let *them* raise the children as they see fit. What is worse is when the government instructed the educational providers to teach **'Humanism'** in our schools. That's the teachings of 'If it feels good, do it. If you want it, take it'. This is a society of people who are bent on 'feeling good about themselves' and as a result they have forgotten all about the little lives they have brought into this world. What we are seeing today is the product of "Humanism". We not only need to take our children back, we need to take our schools back."

I add, "The government has taken over our lives without our permission, and we just throw our hands in the air and say, "Gee, what can I do? Well, no more. It is time to do something about it. Chance, you and I and the entire team are going to try to put a stop to this "zombie world" we are becoming, or we will die trying."

Again, everyone applauds.

"Chauncey, I've been meaning to bring this up to you but never had the opportunity until now," Uncle Miltie says. "My eldest son, Carl, came home from school one day and he was in a terrible snit. His History teacher was making a point about WW 2, and Carl raised his hand and called him on it. He said the teacher was wrong and he quoted what really happened." Milton went on, "The teacher got so angry, he sent Carl to the principal's office and the principal sent Carl home." Milton continues, "Now, I want to know just what we can do about the crap they are teaching our children in school."

"I sure wish I had the answer for you Miltie, but just like we have been saying, until we get the government out of our schools and out of our lives, there isn't a whole hell of a lot we can do. Make sure your children read, read, read. They will learn a lot more by reading than anything else. Of course you could go to the school and inform them of the facts, but then you will probably just make it harder for Carl." Chance asks, "What grade is Carl in, Milton?"

"He was a junior, when that happened," Milton answers. "I went to the school to have a talk with the principal and I got the run-around. Carl has always been fascinated with World War 2 and he has read just about every book ever published on the subject. It really made him angry when the teacher was giving wrong information to the students."

Chance answers, "That's exactly what I've been saying for years. Why do we allow the government to run our schools?" "We really need to get back to basics and see that the right information is being taught to our children." "We can't allow the government to make up history as they want us to see it." Chance says. "We have been giving way too much power to the government. In the words of Lord Acton's writings back in 1887, "Power tends to corrupt. Absolute power corrupts absolutely."

Chance continues, "We elect a Politian and instead of doing the peoples bidding, they let their egos take over and they stop listening to the people and start pushing their own agenda; an agenda the voting public did not choose. We need to start asking the right questions of the Politian when they are asking for our vote. The media, i.e. Television, takes over and everything is staged so the TV station can increase their ratings. The Media is not interested in knowing what a Politian is all about. They are only interested in ratings."

Chance apologizes for going on and on about the government, but he just can't stop, once he gets started. He gets very angry with people who just sit and allow the government to slowly take their freedoms away.

Hank says, "Don't apologize, Chauncey, I think we all need to be reminded once in a while about how and why this great country was formed. It was actually formed by Statesmen not Politicians as we seem to have now. And always remember, our Country is a Republic, not a Democracy."

Everyone agrees and they give each other a hug and say their good nights. The hour is late and the men have a lot to do the next day. Miltie shakes Chance's hand and says, "Thanks for making us think. We need to be reminded now and then just what we are here for. This is a great Country and I don't like to see anyone take advantage of our freedoms or destroy our freedoms or our way of life."

"Thank you for putting up with my tirade," Chance says. They give each other a big hug and say good night.

Chance and I clean up the dishes. Chance says, "That was a wonderful desert you served tonight, Sweetheart."

"Thanks, that was one of my mother's recipes. It has always been a favorite in my family."

"What do you call it," Chance asked.

"You know, I don't really know if it has a name...it must have...I just call it "Strawberry Cream Cake"." My mother used to make that cake for everyone's birthday. "It is made with Angel Food cake, Jell-O, whipped cream, and fresh strawberries. It is really very simple to make. That's why I made it, because I didn't have very much time."

"I love strawberries," Chance said. "I will eat anything so long as it has strawberries on it," he added.

"I love them too, although, I don't think I would eat them on just anything," I say with a grin.

Chance laughs and says, "You know Laura, I really enjoyed this little rap session we had tonight. We need to do that more often. It really felt good to get that stuff off my chest."

"I know the feeling, sweetheart. It's good to have a rap session once in a while, to air things that are on your mind." They head toward the door. "Good night, Mr. Sinclair, I adore you, see you in the morning."

Chance gives me a kiss and says, "Good night, Mrs. Sinclair, I love you." He adds with a wink, "Wouldn't you like me to stay a little longer. I have an awful lot of energy I would like to get rid of before I retire."

"I thought you would never ask, my darling," I answer. Another. .

<u>FADE TO BLACK</u>.

Chapter XXI

THE PREPARATION

Chance gets an early start in the morning, as he has another meeting with Charles. When he returns he fills me in. "When I met with Charles I tried to get more information out of him about what is going on. I didn't have much luck. For some reason, Charles is very tight lipped about his next move. I am hoping he isn't on to us about our plan to destroy him."

Chance is mad as hell. He says, "Charles and his colleagues are not happy with production and that perhaps we shouldn't be so fussy with our eliminations."

I come back, "Gosh, let's start sending him deformed fetuses, then his little 'Perfect Society' wouldn't be so perfect after all."

I think better of that idea. "Knowing the attitude of these ghouls, after bringing the fetuses to maturity, they would probably torture them to death, because they aren't 'perfect'."

Chance calls the team together again. We meet at the same wooded area where I was brought into the group officially. It turns out that it really is a very isolated area and perfect for our long meetings. Ironically everyone in the group thinks exactly the way Chance and I do about the way things are going in the government and the Country. Chance and his team know that Charles and a few of his colleagues are doing this all on their own. They are using government funds to support their experiments and their scientific objectives. They know that the government is guilty of taking liberties with the well being of its citizens once in a while, but they also know the government isn't into these types of experiments. I, on the other hand, am not privy to this information for a while yet.

Chance tells us that he thinks Charles is getting ready to move himself and his cohorts to the compound in Wyoming. "He seemed very anxious to get as many fetuses as can be shipped to him," Chance says. "I'm not sure exactly when he is going, but I'm sure it will be soon. We are going to have to make our move as soon as possible. I want to be sure that all of you are ready both mentally and physically."

Uncle Miltie says, "I think I can speak for all of us, Chauncey, we are ready as we'll ever be." All of the men agree and the wives nod and give the thumbs up.

Our plans are finalized and I tell the clinic that I have to go home because my mother is very ill. I telephone Mother and try to fill her in without really giving anything away. I tell her to go to bed, just in case they show up to verify everything. Mother is used to my strange requests because after being involved with the government for as long as she has, she learned not to ask too many questions. Being a military wife, she has never questioned anything.

I tell Mother about my marriage to Chance. She says she remembers him and is very pleased. She met him when she came to visit me while I was still in Bethesda with the government. She said she is happy for me because he seemed like such a nice man.

I said, "Yes Mom, he is a very nice man and we love each other very much. We will try to get home real soon for a visit. I love you Mom," I said just before I hang up the phone.

#

There are four children in my family. Our father died at the young age of 55, and our mother raised all four of us by herself. We are three girls and one boy; Lee, Larry, me, and Lou Ann.

Lee is the oldest. She is in the modeling business in New York. She has traveled all over the world. Lee retired from modeling when she was 39 years old and started her own, very successful, modeling agency.

Lou Ann is the youngest and is married to George Preston. They have two daughters and a son. Lou Ann and her family live in Madison, Wisconsin. George owns and operates a computer Company.

Brother Larry lives in California, and produces television shows. Larry is married to Judy, and they have five children. I am next to the youngest.

We all try to get together at least once a year, just to torment each other. When they meet Chance, they all fall, instantly, in love with him. Chance is the kindest, gentlest man I have ever known. Lee said she would give up her career if she could find a man like Chance. I'm sure glad I found him first. Lee is beautiful, tall and slim. She too takes after Daddy, as she is a very handsome woman.

Daddy was a highly decorated Lieutenant General in the Army. Gerald Walter Willows (his friends called him G.W.), graduated from West Point and entered the Army as 1st Lieutenant. He was very tall, with a physique like a Greek God. Whenever he entered a room, a hush would come over the crowd. He was breathtakingly handsome, especially in his uniform. All eyes would be on him as he walked down a street, entered a department store or restaurant. He retired as a Lieutenant Colonel after 20 years of service. He re-upped for 10 more years and was promoted to Brigadier General, and was then promoted to Lieutenant General, when he again retired, this time for good. He was a friend to several presidents.

President Eisenhower was my granddaddy's superior officer during World War II. In 1945 Granddaddy was assigned to Shape Headquarters in Paris, France, when the Enola Gay was sent to drop the Atomic Bomb on Hiroshima, Japan. This was the end of the Second World War.

Daddy retired from the Army the second time when he was 53 years old; two years later, he died of a massive heart attack. Daddy is buried at Arlington Cemetery alongside of his father. At his funeral he was given a 21 gun Salute. Daddy had several medals for bravery in action. His father was in the Battle of the Bulge and was awarded the Congressional Medal of Honor. He received a Silver Star for bravery during the invasion in France at the Omaha Beachhead. He had a Distinguished Service Cross for action during World War II.

I was 13 years old when Daddy died. After his death, our mother, Helen, moved all of us to Indianapolis, Indiana, where she had a job with the government.

When President Reagan heard that I graduated from John's Hopkins with honors, and was interning at the Medical Center, he asked the bureau if they had a spot for me in one of their biomedical labs. They did and I was hired. President Reagan said he wanted me working for the government because he wanted people he could trust, doing the technical and important tasks. I was honored that President Reagan had that much faith in the daughter of Gerald Willows.

Mother, Helen Willows, is a thin wisp of a woman. She never remarried after Daddy died. She dated a couple of men about 10 years into her widowhood, but she just couldn't bring herself to marry anyone else. She was devastated when Daddy had his heart attack. He never had any signs of heart trouble. Mother is full of energy and always has a smile for a stranger. She is very supportive of all her children in everything we want to do. If we are ever caught doing something bad or illegal, however, she would say, in her words, "I will knock you to a peak and knock the peak off." We never really knew what that meant, but we knew she meant business when she said it. With Mother, it is black or white, no gray areas. You are either right or wrong. There is no maybe with her. Mother also has a saying that she repeats a few times whenever we thought she was being too strict. She said, "As a teenager, I have walked in your shoes; as a parent, you have not yet walked in mine." I actually thought that was very profound and I heeded her meaning.

#

Getting back to our important plans. As it turns out, 'THEY' were never even watching Chance and me. We didn't have to do all that sneaking around after all. Charles was more interested in his experiments than what Chance and I were up to. They aren't as efficient as we thought; or they trusted Chance and me more than they should have. Either way, we make sure no mistakes are made. We can ill afford to screw this up.

Somewhere along the way the "geniuses" at the Experiment Lab get a little carried away with their power and everything gets out of hand. No one is really sure just who started this whole thing that Chance and I were about to expose. I think it was probably Charles because of the way he has appointed himself as the overseer of the entire project.

The only way we can figure is they are concentrating so hard on their devious scheme, they didn't give much thought to what Chance and I are doing. Either that or they trusted us to be submissive to their scheme.

"They probably assumed that we would blindly follow their orders and not question anything. They just didn't know with whom they were dealing," I emphasize to Chance one day. I would have loved to slap that smug smirk off of Charles Knight's face when he approached me about all this. At the time, however, I thought I was alone in this mess or I would have.

"You know, sweetheart, I don't know what I would have done if you hadn't been so against what was going on." Chance confessed, "I was pretty sure that you would be with me, because I know what a decent person you are. When Charles asked me if I would be interested in this assignment I hesitated at first, then I thought, no, now that I know Laura is being pushed into this I'm sure she will be as disgusted as I am about this whole thing."

I said, "You were right to think that. Actually I had a bitter-sweet reaction when you turned out to be my contact. I was glad to see you again but sad that you were my contact. I always thought you were a decent person too." I added, "I sure am glad things turned out the way they did. I Love you and respect you so much."

"My Lady, You have my vote for 'Citizen of the Year'."

Chapter XXII

ONE LAST COOK-OFF

It's time for one last "cook-off" before our trip, and it's my turn. I was cooking for only part of the team. Some of the men were busy getting all the gear ready for traveling.

#

I had a roommate in Medical School named Harriet Pappas who was of Greek descent. I think her last name was short for something else, but I wouldn't be able to pronounce it anyway. Harriet was and still is my best friend. I used to go home with her a lot on weekends and some Holidays. Harriet lived a lot closer to School than I. She came home with me on Christmas break one year because her parents had to go to Greece on some family business. Her two brothers, who are much older than she, went to Greece with their parents that year. Harriet is the one who introduced me to Greek cuisine.

I went home with Harriet for Easter one year. Her mother was a terrific cook and she put on a spread that sent me into 'Dining Heaven'. Easter is a big Holiday in the Greek Church and family. They all go to Midnight Mass and after the services everyone is invited over to the house for a feast. It is the first full meal after 40 days of fasting. When the Greeks fast during Lent, they eat no blood animal. Their diet consists mainly of seafood and vegetables. I receive several recipes from Harriet's mother. Harriet has to translate some of the ingredients as her mother speaks very broken English and knows some of the words only in Greek.

Harriet married a doctor from Greece and they moved there to live. She has three beautiful children. She sends pictures from time to time. They have a wonderful life in Greece.

#

I learned how to make some great dishes after watching Harriet's mother prepare some of her meals. I serve an authentic Greek meal to Chance and the others that night. The meal starts with egg and lemon soup, called Avgolemeno Soupa. A delicious Greek salad is served next. Roast Greek chicken with lemon and roasted potatoes are served for the main course. I even make a Greek dessert. Harriet's mother taught me how to make Crème Caramella, baked custard with Carmel sauce. I had to make two custards to serve to everyone. Greek food is my favorite cuisine; however, it takes just about all day to prepare one meal. It was a miracle that I got all this accomplished with no interruptions. No wonder Harriet's mother never learned much English; she spent all her time in the kitchen cooking for her family.

"Holidays are very big events in the Greek homes. Instead of birthdays, they celebrate 'Name Days'. Their 'Name Day' is the Saint for whom they were named." I tell Chance, "You will not believe the spread this woman puts out for her husband's 'Name Day'. She not only cooks all the Greek foods, she also has several American dishes including Lobster Newburg. What a Feast!"

Chance says, "I am now convinced that Greek cuisine is my favorite. That was a marvelous meal Laura. Thank you. My hat is off to you for taking the time to cook this wonderful experience."

Everyone joins in and thanks me for going to the trouble of preparing such a great feast. I was very proud that everything turned out okay. "You are welcome. It is a pleasure cooking for all of you," I said.

Everyone had two helpings of everything. Boy, how those men can eat; and their weights stay the same. They must have a very high metabolism. After that meal I had to go on a diet for a week.

Everyone enjoyed the dessert. Trudy said it is very similar to Flan, which is her favorite dessert.

"Greek cuisine, I will admit, is my favorite food." I love everything except one dish that they make at Easter. It is a stew like dish made from Lamb intestines. I had to pass on that one."

Later that evening Chance receives the maps from Ian. He did an excellent job I thought. What detail. We plan the entire attack from these maps. I mentioned guns earlier and how most of us are marksmen. We don't want anyone to think that we are going into this thing with killing in mind. Killing anyone is the farthest thing from our minds. We are not mercenaries. We are just trying to keep our country in good stead.

The only reason guns are brought into this is because Chance noticed that the compound had armed guards. As it turns out, they have more artillery than even Chance detected. We need to protect ourselves and if we need to kill someone, well, then we will have to kill someone. None of us are looking forward to killing anyone. Especially me, I have only shot at targets before I came on board with Chance. When push comes to shove though, I'm pretty sure I can hold my own.

"It's a good thing the Constitution of the United States allows us to bear arms," Chance says. "Without our guns, we would be helpless in resolving this atrocity. If the "bleeding hearts" have their way, we will be helpless to defend any of our freedoms." Chance continues, "This is what Adolf Hitler did in Germany and Poland during his reign. He took all the guns away from the citizens and left them defenseless to protect themselves against the Nazi Regime. Actually, if it really comes down to whom is to blame for the Holocaust; I will have to say it was the Jews themselves. Now, this will anger some people, and I'm sure I will get an argument from a lot of you; but if you think about it you might agree. The Jews, in wanting to be good citizens and not make waves, handed over all their personal weapons to Hitler's henchmen. Not that they really had a choice. They had no way of defending themselves against the atrocities that followed. We Americans must always fight to keep our freedoms. The same thing could happen in this country if we aren't careful. We must pay attention to what is going on in Washington at all times. Responsible people should not have to pay for irresponsible people's stupidity. They need to start punishing the **guilty** not the **innocent**."

"You have an excellent point Chauncey," Tom says. "I tend to agree with that concept now that I think about it. That could very possibly happen in this country, if we let the ball drop on this one."

"If certain politicians have their way, we will be in that same boat." Chance says. "Always stand up for your Rights, no matter what. Don't let anyone bully you into thinking otherwise."

"After our little Rap session the other night, I am fully aware of what is going on around us. Believe me, Chance, I will do everything in my power to keep our freedoms and hang on to our rights," I add.

Chance says in a quizzical manner, "What disturbs me more than anything is that certain politicians are privy to all our military and government secrets? I'm wondering if or how many of our secrets they have sold to other nations. Some politicians certainly seem to have unlimited funds."

"Wow, that's very profound." I say.

Chapter XXIII

THE TRIP WEST

Chance contacts Wayne and the wheels are set in motion for our arrival in Wyoming. We think better of descending upon Wyoming in full force, so we leave Worcester, in staggered shifts. A few of the guys fly out first to help Wayne get things set up. Next, Ian and Carmel, leave in their van. Mickey and Terry Healy, go with them.

I invite the men and their wives over for dessert. Chance and I eat early while the men were doing the last minute checks on all the equipment. Toni and Carol pick up the two rented vans that we need. Toni orders burgers and salads for everyone as they work at Chances apartment.

Wherever Ian and Carmel go, Mickey and Terry aren't far behind. Mickey still has his climbing trips with Steve; Ian can't join them for that, but Mickey is seldom apart from Ian for any length of time.

We need special equipment for the mountains and the unknown terrain, and it can only be taken by van. We drive five vans. The vans are the first to leave for Wyoming. Some of the men leave on staggered flights; sort of what Chance and I did when we flew to Wyoming the first time.

Chance and I drive the last van. We bring up the rear, in case anyone has trouble, we will be there to help out. Joe Falkner is in the van just ahead of ours. In case anyone has engine trouble he will be on hand to help. We have specific points where we will stop. If anyone has any mishaps with a flat tire or anything, they will wait for the next van to arrive whether it is at the designated stop or along the roadside. We make sure everyone is well rested before anyone does any driving.

We keep in contact with each other by cell phones, throughout the entire trip. Talk is in code most of the time, as cell phones can be monitored.

Everyone pools his or her cash and it is divided between each group in each van, so we all have enough money on the trip for gas, food, lodging and any emergency that might crop up. We don't want anyone using a credit card, for security reasons. At least two couples go in each van. Chip and Trudy join Joe in his van. We don't take the chance that anyone will become tired while driving.

The guys who don't have their wives with them fly out, unless they are needed for a specific task on the road. It looks better for husband and wife teams to be driving rather than a bunch of men all piled in a van.

I said, "Chance, you have thought of every little detail."

"Let's hope I have, Laura. . .let's hope I have."

Chance is always so afraid that someone might get hurt if he makes a mistake in the planning. It will take at least three days to get to our destination in Wyoming. We want no speeding along the way. We can ill afford to be stopped by a highway patrolman. With the kind of equipment we are carrying, there will be a lot of explaining to do if caught. The men are all very good and conscientious drivers, and they know how important this mission is. We make sure every van's headlights, taillights, breaks and everything else are working properly. We double-check everything.

Joe Faulkner is in charge of the vehicles. If there is anything mechanically wrong with any of them, he will find it and fix it. Each van is equipped with new tires. Joe purchases extra tires. He puts the extra tires in his van, just in case someone has a flat tire on the way to Wyoming. The vans take various tire sizes, so he purchases them accordingly.

As Chance and I are about to leave Worcester, guess who joins us? "Cora!" I yell, "What the hell are you doing here?"

Chance looks at me with a sheepish grim and said, "Cora's with me, sweetheart."

Cora says, "You think I wouldn't actually work for a creep like that pompous, narcissistic, boob Charles, do you?" Cora hugs me, picks me up and swings me around as if I was a rag doll. Cora says, "I thought for sure you were on to me. That's why I jumped all over you that day. Chauncey wanted my identity kept quiet so I could get information that you could not. He also was being cautious about our friendship. He thought if you knew who I was, we might become a little lax in our conversations around the others."

I start to stutter and reply, "Chance, you mean. . .all this time. . .and I was worried that I would have to turn her in. . .does she know we are married and everything?"

"Yup," was his reply.

"And I tried so hard to keep from screaming it from the roof-tops," I said. "If you ever keep a secret like this from me again. . .I will murder you both." "Glad to have you aboard, Cora," I say with a smile. I was quite relieved to know that Cora was on our side. She is definitely the type you want on your side, and at your side.

Cora adds, "The only regret I have is that I had to miss out on your initiation ceremony and your wedding. I had a heck of a time keeping from blurting out, 'CONGRATULATIONS'."

"I'll make it up to you, Cora, you can be Godmother to our first born," I promise.

"You're on," Cora comes back.

Outside of stopping every 2 hours or so, the trip to Wyoming is welcomingly uneventful. Every time Cora sees a sign that even hints that there is food in the vicinity, she insists on stopping to eat. She will pat herself on the stomach and announce, "I have to keep this fed or I will just fade away."

I say, "Can't have that now, can we?" I wished that I hadn't been so snippy to Cora at the clinic. I tried to avoid her as much as possible. That was a hard task to do because I liked her so much. I was so afraid that she would catch on that I really wasn't on Charles' side, that I sometimes over did my acting. I agree with Chance in thinking that keeping me in the dark was the best choice at that time.

While we motor to Wyoming, Cora and I become closer than two people can without actually being related. Cora is a delight. I'm certainly glad she is with us. As everyone finds out soon enough, she is one "tuff cookie". No one gets in Cora's way.

Cora makes a profound statement when we start talking about the abortion clinic. We are discussing how, when not too long ago, abortions were illegal, did legalized abortions start; and when and why did they start? Cora says, "Perhaps it's the governments' way of 'ethnic cleansing' without anyone actually coming right out and saying it. When you see how many African Americans and young girls from very poor families are getting abortions, it makes you think."

"Maybe you are on to something, Cora," Chance says.

I add, "I noticed we were never allowed to send any African- American fetuses to them." I recall, "At the time I didn't question their motives for their requests, but I'm certainly having second thoughts about it now." "One African American fetus did slip through, however, through no fault of ours," I said. "A white girl came in and she said she didn't know who the father was. You remember her, don't you Cora?"

Cora nods and says, "Oh, yah, I remember her. I wanted to take her across my knee and wallop some sense into her. The very idea. . .fifteen years old and pregnant."

I continue, "The girl more or less acted like she didn't know who the father was. I thought she was trying to protect him from being prosecuted for statutory rape because of her age. She did let it slip, at one point, that the father was 19 years old. That fetus was sent to Wyoming."

I found out several weeks later that the boyfriend was black. "It will be interesting to see if any of the children, at the compound, are black, Perhaps they perfected my skin pigmentation experiments. I worked on taking certain pigments out of skin tones. I never had the chance to test Negro pigment. That will definitely be one of the things we look into when we get there; provided our plans work out in our favor."

We are about an hour into our journey when Chance becomes very serious and he says, "Darling, there is one more thing that we have kept from you, and I need to tell you about it now, and I need your understanding and support."

"Oh, my," I said with a lump in my throat, "You sound so serious, what is it, Chance? Are you going to tell me that we really aren't married?"

He says, "No, Honey, nothing like that. Cora, my Army buddies, and I are secret agents working for an organization called the "National Independent Covert Action", or N.I.C.A. We are on the staff and we answer only to our boss, who, in turn, answers to the head of the CIA. It's a little difficult to actually explain just what the N.I.C.A. is." Chance says, "Try to think of it as a part of the government that no one knows about. By no one, I mean no one other than all of us, of course and the Director of the CIA. Our contact is known to us only by his code name, "Phantom". None of us knows "Phantom's" real name. We only know him as "Phantom". There is a secret phone number that only I know. That is the only way I have of communicating with him. We can go places and do things that no one else can. The CIA formed the N.I.C.A, as a sort of secret watchdog for everything that goes on in the government. If the government screws up one of their projects, the N.I.C.A. intervenes and corrects it or makes it go away. If the government squeaks, we oil it. We more or less, keep the government honest. At least we try to keep them honest. That way the government ends up with clean hands and no one is the wiser. In this case, however, Charles and his cronies are on their own. They have taken it upon themselves to experiment on these fetuses. Actually, now that I think about it, I'll bet some of the others don't even know that they are **not** doing this for the government. This could be all

Charles' doing and knowing him, he, and maybe two or three of the other doctors, could be keeping the rest of them in the dark."

Chance continues, "We, meaning Cora, the other men and myself, have been around since the Vietnam War. Before our team was formed it was a different group of men from a different war. The government always picks men from a certain well-groomed unit of the service. They happened to select this group because of our loyalty to our country and our grit. We are very well paid for what we do and we keep the gears of this country well oiled." "You see," Chance says, "Just because someone says something against the government does not mean he or she is being disloyal to his or her country. On the contrary, the **people** make up a country, and the people **are** the government." Chance adds, "This project got out of hand. Now we have to go in and correct it. The government actually started the whole thing, but they didn't keep their finger on the pulse and the people who were put in charge, namely Dr. Charles Knight, took advantage of the situation. As a result, the egomaniac went too far. Now we have to go in and clean house."

Cora says, "We only kept all this from you to protect you. The less you knew at first the better off you were."

I was silent for a while as I tried to absorb what I just heard. "I'm curious, does this mean that I wasn't working for the government, but I was working for Charles?"

Chance says, "Not really, but you could put it that way. You see when I came to the Lab Facility, four years before you arrived, I was onto Charles and so was the CIA. At that time the CIA didn't actually know who was running the show, but they had a suspicion that it was Charles. They also needed to know who else was involved. Questions arose as to the expenditures that were coming out of the lab." Chance continues as the veins in his neck tense up, "I'm sure the government actually had this project in mind but not to the extent Charles has taken it. The government definitely wants to pursue the Stem-Cell side of medicine. So you were doing government work, but Charles sneaked in some of his own projects, unbeknownst to you or anyone else."

"Wow, this is mind boggling," I say with a huge sigh. "This would also explain your camaraderie with all your friends," I said. "Your lives depend on your closeness and love for each other."

Cora chimes in, "You bet it does, Laura, and I think you already have that same love in you, that Chauncey and I have for the men and their wives. When Chauncey asked me to join the staff of your lab, I jumped at the chance to nail Charles once I heard what he was suspected of doing."

"You're right, Cora, I do love those men and their wives. I have never met a group of people with the kindness and compassion that they all seem to have. And I'm so glad you are part of the group. The CIA knew what they were doing when they picked this team."

As events of the passed few months do a replay in my mind, I can now put everything into perspective. Everything makes more sense now. The Ceremony, the comrade-ship, everything falls into place.

"So, as I see it, this has nothing to do with the government so much as it has to do with Charles and his partners in crime?" I queried.

"That's right sweetheart. We have to put a stop to Charles and his cohorts before the government gets a black eye. Hopefully we can put a stop to this without any publicity," Chance adds.

"My hat is off to you Cora. I thought I was a good actress, but you take the Oscar," I said.

Chance says, "This whole situation came about when a handful of scientists took it upon themselves to play God. Some of them think they are God. There is Drs. Charles Knight, Clyde Kenner, Madelyn Schultz and Homer Van Elsten. These doctors were the 'King-Pins'. Dr. Knight wanted everything covert, so he chose the government owned land in Wyoming. He knew there wouldn't be any interference from outsiders because it was so isolated. The government more or less closed their eyes and let the scientists take over. The scientists had free rein because "Big Daddy" wasn't looking. When the cat's away..."

"By the time the CIA looked into it, everything was already in place and paid for with our tax dollars." Chance explains. "The government had no idea what was going on. No one took the time to check up on these scientists. The CIA had suspicions that some doctors at the Center were into more than they were supposed to be. That's when I was sent there to check into things. This is where we all come into play."

"The government doesn't want egg on their face or have to explain their stupidity as to why they didn't keep a closer eye on things," Cora adds.

Chance says, "At first I thought everything to be normal. It wasn't until those two scientists were poisoned, Laura, that I became more suspicious. Charles was very good at covering up his actions. The N.I.C.A asked me to pay close attention and play into Charles' hands. That way, if I act like I'm with him in what he and his cohorts are doing, I can infiltrate his group."

"The entire time I worked for this project, I had no idea that anything of this magnitude was in progress. They certainly kept everything to themselves," I said.

"A typical government maneuver, the right hand never knows what the left hand is doing, so Charles got away with charging ahead on his devious plan." Chance answered.

Chance continued, "I put my team on alert just before I contacted you, for the first time." Chance is the team's leader and if he can't handle things alone, he calls on his comrades to help out. This mission needs all of them. Sometimes Chance and his covert unit have to go against the government and its dealings. "We are also the watchdogs of the Constitution of the United States. When the citizen's rights are being abused, we try to set things straight. We have our work cut out for us, and we try to keep up on things as quietly as we can without ruffling too many feathers," Chance said.

Chance adds, "I thought for sure I gave it all away when I was talking about how this team would be eliminated if some of the politicians and money people knew about us. I was hoping you didn't catch that 'faux pas'."

"I never gave it a second thought. I guess it went right over my head." I said.

"Everything starts to make more sense to me now. I was a little curious as to why everything seemed to fall into place without so much as a "chink" in any of our plans. Up until now I just thought you were all that good. This group really has great affection for one another, however, that part isn't a sham." I add. "Your love and respect for each other is very genuine."

"So, tell me, Cora, where did you take your acting lessons?" I ask, with a smirk on her face.

"The same place you did, smart ass," Cora comes back. We give each other a jab and laugh.

Chance says, "I was given permission to include you in the operation, as I told "Phantom" that I am going to marry you and that I will leave the N.I.C.A. if I'm not allowed to bring you into my confidence." I find out that the rest of the men also threatened to quit if I was not brought on board. "I am honored, sweetheart, that you and everyone have so much faith in me," I said.

"You mean you aren't angry that I didn't bring you into my confidence earlier?" He asked.

"Of course not," I answered, "I have lived with the government long enough to know how important it is to keep a clandestine atmosphere."

Cora chimes in and says, "I was all for telling you the minute I met you, but we had to wait for the okay from the 'big guy'. It made what we had to do a lot easier."

"After this is all over, Laura, we will never speak of this project again, not openly anyway." Chance added. I understood completely.

Chapter XXIV

MENDING FENCES

When Chance wanted to talk to Wayne alone at his cabin he told him about his involvement with the N.I.C.A., and asked him if he would be interested in joining him and his men. He told Wayne, whether he joined them or not he would have to be sworn to secrecy about their existence. Wayne said, "I am honored that you have enough faith in me to ask me for your help." Chance had already cleared it with "Phantom" to involve Wayne in this caper. "Phantom" knew all about Wayne's so called "Dishonorable Discharge", and welcomed the opportunity to repay him for his patriotism. He even took it upon himself to have all Wayne's records changed to show that he had received an "honorable discharge", and that he has the full benefits from being in the Armed Services.

Wayne told Chance that perhaps this would redeem him in Rose's eyes, because he never told her the truth and he never stopped loving her. He said he often wondered what happened to her.

#

What Wayne didn't know was that when this was all over, Chance and I put out feelers to find Rose. We had a lead that Rose was living in Denver. She opened a little cafe and lives alone. Chance and I fly to Denver and stop in to see her. She never forgave herself for not standing by Wayne when he needed her most. She often wanted to get in touch with him but had no idea where to reach him. She said she just couldn't handle the disgrace and shame of his dishonorable discharge. She said Wayne became very distant and wouldn't talk about anything to her, just that he was dishonorable discharged. She said she didn't think she had any other choice but to leave him. We explain to her what happened, in truth, and she wants to see Wayne again and ask for his forgiveness. After we tell her that Wayne never stopped loving her; her face lights up and she asks us to, please, take her to him.

Rose is a very shy yet a personable woman. She isn't at all worldly like you would expect, being married to someone like Wayne. She dresses very simply and wears no makeup, except very pale lipstick. She wears her hair cut short so she doesn't have to fuss with it. She isn't very tall, about 5' 2", and just a few pounds over weight. She carries herself as if she has height. Her posture is perfect.

It is a fantastic reunion. Everyone is assembled in our private wooded area for a picnic. The men have taken Wayne to a barber and had him trimmed up so he looks like his old self. Chance and I bring Rose with us, as we arrived late.

When their eyes meet, they run to each other and Wayne lifts Rose into his arms and swings her around and around. It is a very moving moment; and as I look around with tears in my eyes, everyone is crying. Wayne and Rose get remarried at the same Justice of the Peace in Auburn, Mass., where Chance and I were united. Wayne looks at Chance, gives him a 'wink and a nod' and they know each other's thoughts without saying a word.

Chapter XXV

REMINISCING

The rest of our trip to Wyoming is mostly spent planning our strategy. We do get in a few laughs, however, when Cora's stomach gives out a GRRROWL. Thank God we are able to laugh once in a while. We will go bonkers if there isn't some levity. This whole ordeal is a terrible strain on everyone. When it is all over we can see the toll it takes on all our faces.

I said, "I really am sorry, Cora. I wasn't very nice to you sometimes at the clinic. I really like you and it bothered me that I had to grumble at you."

"No apology necessary," Cora says. "If you had been nicer, I would have had to be nastier, so I wouldn't blow my cover; and that fence would have been very difficult to mend. That's one of the reasons I didn't want Chauncey telling you about me. I wanted you to play your role exactly the way you did."

"I know exactly what you mean pal," I said.

It looks like Chance is getting ready to scratch his head on that one, but then something must have kicked in, as he starts to nod his head as if to say, "Oh, now I get it." His mind is on other things.

"What are you thinking about, Chance?" Cora asks.

"I'm just thinking about the men and their wives and how important this mission is to all of us. I guess I'm silently praying that no one will be hurt or killed." Chance is the type of person who will blame himself for anyone's injuries or death.

"I'm thinking about another mission my unit and I were on. It was a much deadlier mission than this. We were in Vietnam. I was leading my men into an ambush and didn't know it. The enemy infiltrated our base and information was given to the base commander that the North Vietnamese High Command would be in this one particular area. My unit was chosen to go in and capture them. The enemy was waiting in ambush and half of my unit was killed. I grieve for those men to this day."

#

Uncle Miltie says, "He is always too hard on himself. He actually saved the lives of the other men, because of his quick thinking and expeditious actions."

Uncle Miltie talks about Jim Jefferies, who was in Chance's unit at that time. "Jim told me about how Chauncey saved the rest of them. He said Chauncey had a block of plastic explosive; he attached a live hand-grenade to it and threw it at a tree about 30 yards away from them; and right in the middle of the enemy. The plastic stuck to the tree and that was the end of that enemy unit. Jim was one of the team up until a few years ago. He chose to leave the team because his wife became very ill and he needed to be with her and help her through her illness. His wife had a nervous breakdown and Jim stayed by her side until she was well again."

Willie adds, "If Chauncey hadn't had his wits about him, we all would have been killed. Because of his acumen for detail and his cognizance of everything around him, we are all still here."

Chauncey has been the predominant leader of our group. No one has ever second-guessed him in his decision-making. It is really a culmination of everyone's efforts to reach perfection that makes Chauncey and the rest of us so in-tune to each other."

#

When the trip starts to get boring we get on the subject of our favorite movies. Cora says, "Gone With The Wind" is the best movie ever made." Of course, we all agree on that.

Chance said, "My favorite movies are Westerns, especially the ones with John Wayne in them."

"Why doesn't that come as a surprise to me?" I said. "My all time favorite Movie is "An Affair to Remember", with Cary Grant and Deborah Kerr."

Chance teases, "That figures, you are such a romantic."

"My all time favorite line in a movie is from "The Marriage-Go-Round", with Susan Hayward and James Mason." I go on to explain, "Susan's character thinks she has caught her husband, James Mason, having a liaison with Julie Newmar, who is the young sexy daughter of a colleague from Sweden, who is staying with them; and Susan says to her husband, "I came; I saw; I frowed up". "I love that line!" I said. "Susan Hayward has always been my favorite Actress."

Cora hadn't seen that film and when I said that line, she laughed for the next 50 miles.

Chance has a great memory for famous John Wayne lines. He repeats lines from just about every movie John Wayne was in. He even has his voice pattern down pat. I'm sure learning a lot about Chance on this trip. If you really want to learn all about a person, just take a motor trip with them. We talk about great lines from the movies until we have to stop for the day and get motel rooms.

When Cora, Chance, and I arrive at Wayne's cabin, everyone is there. A few of them are used to sleeping in their Vans, so the limited accommodations are no problem. We are glad that Wayne's cabin is out of the way so no one has any suspicion of any strange activity that is going on with all of us there. Even though Wayne has had many over-night visitors; he has never had this many all at once.

Just before we enter Wayne's cabin I take a deep breath and exclaim, "I have never smelled such clean air as is in these mountains. The air here is intoxicating."

Cora says, "You are right, I could stay here for the rest of my life and just inhale."

Wayne, Chance and Bobby Joe take a ride in the helicopter to take one last survey of the area to see if there is any way to approach the compound other than by air. They also want to make sure there is no activity in the area. Chance says, "Perhaps there might be an obscure road somewhere that may have been missed on our first approach." His hunch is correct. There is a very small and winding road that looks like it was made with mules or on horseback. Actually, Ian drew the path on his maps; we just aren't paying attention.

Ian and Carmel are already at the lodge, or he could have saved the men the trip. They did need to check out the area for activity; however, as we certainly didn't want to meet up with anyone as we approach the Compound.

Chance checks the weather report and he tells us that clouds are rolling in from the west and could possibly hinder our way up the mountain path. "We will play it by ear and see what happens in the morning. I don't want to delay our trip if we can put up with a little drizzle, but if we are up against a down pour it will be a problem.

Everyone sleeps very restlessly that night in anticipation of our journey the next day. Some of them stay up late and play cards to relax. The next morning presents us with heavy cloud cover. It is starting to sprinkle, just a mist more than a sprinkle. We drive as close to our destination as we can with the Vans. We park them at Steve and Joanne's Lodge. The road to the Lodge isn't too bad for a secondary road. It did start to get a little muddy but not bad enough to abort the mission.

Steve and Joanne close the Lodge for the next few months, so we can use it for our Base. They were the first to fly out of Worcester to get things set up for all of us.

We will backpack the rest of the way to the Compound. Ian and Carmel stay at the lodge along with Joanne and another couple, Tom and Carol Brody. They will be the contact Base. We will be in constant radio contact with them. After we leave Wayne's cabin, Tom flies his helicopter to the lodge in case it is needed.

The lodge has a heliport on the property. It is a large facility where many dignitaries and Hollywood types stay because it is out of the way and they can relax and not worry about being hounded by the press. The lodge is situated near Gannett Peak, the highest point in Wyoming (13,804 ft.). It is just west of the continental divide and a spectacular ski area.

As I step out of our vehicle the unsullied mountain air whips passed my face and I take a deep breath and say, "Wow this is the cleanest, freshest air I have ever smelled. I think I could get drunk on this stuff."

Chance replies, "I have always loved the great mountain air. It's so clean and crisp. Be careful Laura, I don't want you drunk." He says with a laugh.

Cora said, "I don't think I have ever smelled anything as healthy as the air up here. It's wonderful. I'm filling my lungs with this stuff and taking it home for future use. I don't even mind the rain."

The lodge is an impressive building that looks like a log cabin. There are three floors plus a basement. In building the basement they had to blast through solid rock. Part of the basement is built into the mountain. Part of the lodge itself is built into the mountain as well. The entire structure was quite an undertaking and took several years to build. The inside is completely insulated; however, they still have the bare beams in the ceiling to look like it isn't insulated. The ceilings are very high and pitched in the entrance hall. There is the feeling we are entering a cathedral. There are 52 Suites and 71 double rooms at the Lodge. During snow season they are always full. Some people ski and some people just come here to relax and get away from it all. During the summer months they cater to groups who love to fish in the clear mountain lakes. If you catch a fish, it is prepared for you at dinner that evening. Steve keeps the lake stocked with blue gills, salmon and bass. There is a beautiful mountain stream that empties into the lake on the north side. Salmon swim up that stream to spawn, so there are always plenty of salmon to catch. The fishermen also have to keep in mind that they are competing with the local bears. A Ranger always accompanies the fishermen just in case they should run into one of those bears.

As usual, there are the elk, moose, deer and buffalo heads on the walls. Steve is a great hunter and whatever he kills; they eat or use the skin for clothing. On the main menu for the restaurant they have buffalo steaks, buffalo burgers, and elk and deer steaks. Joanne also has several soups and stews on the menu made with these same meats. Joanne does all the cooking while the team is there, but they have a chef when they are open to the public. Joanne has other duties to take care of during the skiing season.

Joanne is a well rounded cook. She has an incredible spread waiting for us when we arrive...more of that 'comfort food'. We feast, chat about our next move, go over the plans one more time, and off to bed. The rooms are decorated in a rustic decor; something you would expect at a ski lodge. These are very comfortable quarters. The beds have large feather mattresses, and down comforters. It feels more like home than a hotel. The stairway to the second floor overlooks the entryway. "What an impressive place this is. I think I could get used to this real fast."

Chapter XXVI

THE DISCOVERY

We roll out of bed at 5:00 A.M., have a huge breakfast and are on our way. Joanne has packed sandwiches for us to eat on the trek to the compound. Everyone has his or her own bottles of water. It will take all day to get to the vanguard of the compound.

Some of the equipment is quite heavy. Good thing most of the men are big and muscular. Some of the men may be in their 40's and 50's, but they all stay in great shape; not that we women can't pull our own weight. No one has to carry our loads for us.

The men are armed with rifles and/or handguns. Some of the men have sub-machine guns and some have semi-automatics. Uncle Miltie has a sniper's rifle with telescope. Hank and Bobby Joe are carrying all the explosives.

At one point we have to scale a crag. The weather is still against us. I just hope the temperature doesn't fall or we could be facing a lot of ice. It actually feels a little warmer than it was earlier. The climbers go first and pull the equipment up and then help the rest of us up. Everyone is doing their job and things are going smoothly. The rocks are a little slippery but we are all wearing proper boots so we aren't having too much trouble handling the rocks. The maps that Ian drew are perfect. They are very detailed and easy to follow. It still amazes me just how he drew those maps so accurately just from my photos. We stop periodically to eat, drink and catch our breath. We aren't used to these heights. The path we are following comes to an abrupt halt. We pick it up again when we get closer to the compound.

We approach the compound at night. We study the maps very carefully so we don't lose our way. We stop at intervals to coordinate our next move. We see a lot more artillery at the compound than we had expected. The rain has stopped and we are very thankful for that. "These people are guarding their secret with some heavy stuff. This is serendipitous." Cora whispers.

We use our night-vision glasses in order to see our way to the place that is marked for our stopping point. As we stealthily move closer to the compound, Uncle Miltie can spot a guard off to his left on a mound. They aren't very professional; the guard is smoking a cigarette. Uncle Miltie can make out the guards face from his glowing cigarette butt. Of course, Hank smells the smoke way before any of us know he is there. Hank has already alerted Billy, who immediately jumps into action. We sure are glad that we are more alert than the guards. But then, who is crazy enough to come to this place, anyhow?

We are quite gratified the guards are a little apathetic about their situation. They are easier to take out that way. This is going to make our job of penetration quite a bit easier, hopefully, without much resistance. Or so I thought.

Billy is not only skilled with guns; he is also very adept with knives. He takes out the smoking guard with one of his knives. We wait silently, for a while; to see if anyone is coming to relieve the guard. As morning approaches, we try to stay as unnoticed as possible. We use sign language instead of words, because voices carry in the mountains. A snapped twig can be heard from a block away. We are just below the timber line at this point.

There is a 12 foot, electrified, chain-link fence topped with barbed wire around the Compound. Just before dawn, Steve, Chip and Trudy go on ahead and scale a steep mountain face. They then hang-glide over the fence, into the compound.

They relieve two guards of their weapons and break into their power plant and disconnect the fence. They bind the guards and give them a shot of "knock-out drops". They are very careful not to disconnect any power to the compound. We don't need someone coming out to the Power Station to check on the power. We aren't ready to give our position away just yet.

We were hoping for a little more time than we got, however. Hank cuts his way through the chain link fence and we are able to crawl in through the hole he makes. The rest of the team then enters the compound. Somehow an alarm is triggered, because sirens start whirring. We scurry for cover before we are seen. We all have our weapons drawn. We are ready for anything, but I am silently praying we don't have to kill anyone else.

Some of us are huddled behind a huge bolder. Miltie and the others find a bushy area to hide behind.

Uncle Miltie pops his head up in time to see the guards uncover a Cannon and he sees another guard with a bazooka. Miltie is in his glory. He takes aim at the bazooka and lays one right down the barrel. KABOOM!!!! He takes out the bazooka and the cannon. Chance and I high-five each other and I run over and hug Uncle Miltie. Cora stands there with her mouth wide open. It looks like all we have to do is walk in and take over. Well, not quite. Steve runs to the Power Station and disconnects the siren. By this time we know we have awakened the dead. With the sirens whirring, we couldn't hear any gunshots. There were several guards placed in different areas, who were taking pot shots at us. If we couldn't hear the gunshots then we couldn't tell from which direction they were coming. All of a sudden it felt like everything was going in slow motion. . .the noise. . .the bullets. . .everyone running for cover. My ears were ringing from the explosion and the sirens.

We get a little carried away with our victory over the cannon and bazooka, because we don't notice that Willie Meehan has been hit. No one heard the shot because the sirens were making too much noise. Uncle Miltie saw him go down, that's why he took that pot shot at the bazooka. Willie was standing and looking at the cannon when a guard spotted him and shot him just before everything blew. That guard is no longer on this earth. Cora says, "He's probably orbiting the moon right about now."

When Chance and Mickey Healy get to Willie, he is bleeding badly. Mickey dresses the wound as best he can and Cora radios Toni and Carol to come pick him up with the helicopter. At this point, the heavy artillery is disabled so there will be no danger to Toni and Carol. We check around and all the guards, who were operating the big guns, are dead except for one who is barely breathing. We put him on the helicopter with Willie. He is unconscious, and no threat to anyone. Mickey goes back with Willie so he can take care of him. His Medic training kicks into high gear. The guards who were in the power plant are still out cold. We flush out the rest of the guards who are hiding among the rocks. There are more gunshots exchanged before the helicopter arrives. Uncle Miltie shoots a couple more guards. I think Miltie is mad as hell that Willie was shot. I'm sure he felt he should have disabled the cannon and bazooka sooner. Cora and I are shooting toward the areas where the guards are hiding, but I don't think we hit anyone. I say to Cora, "I hope Uncle Miltie isn't blaming himself for Willie getting shot."

Cora says, "Knowing Miltie, I'm sure he is."

The shooting seems to subside and from what we can see everyone is okay. I say to Cora, "I can't see everyone. Is everyone okay? Can you see them?"

Cora says, "I can't see Billy, but I see Wayne. Wayne looks okay." Chance is looking around and can't see some of the men. We have a signal that we give out if anyone needs help. Chance gives the 'bird whistle', (tweet, tweet, whoot) to receive the distress signal and no one responds. At this point we are presuming everyone is okay. I don't know why no one responded to Chance's call, but because of that we just figured everyone was okay.

Chapter XXVII

OUTLANDISH ACTS

We can't give credence to what is before our own eyes. "It looks like something out of 'Buck Rogers', Bobby Joe says.

There is a huge glass dome, the size of a small town. The compound is self-sufficient, in that they have everything from solar electric power to a sewage system. Inside the dome we find fruit orchards and vegetable gardens. The place is climate controlled, so the occupants don't have to worry about the harsh winters of the Wyoming Mountains. Bobby Joe and Hank have to use some of their plastic explosives to blow the lock on the front door of the Dome. "The doors are enormous and the locks are almost impenetrable." Hank says.

"Perhaps it's impenetrable for an amateur, but certainly not for Bobby Joe and Hank." Cora whispers.

Once we are inside the dome, we encounter more guards. The guards are not prepared for the likes of us. One of the guards was just getting ready to heave a hand grenade at the front door. When the door exploded, he just drops the grenade, with the pin intact, thank goodness. They throw their weapons down and throw their hands up as they see our weaponry pointing right at them. The main building, which is guarded but unlocked, is the focal point of the compound. This is where everything is housed for their experiments. Chance walks over to one of the guards, puts his hand on his shoulder and says, "You all right? Is everything okay?"

The guard, Richard Cummings, says, "Sure Chauncey, what took you so long?" He throws Chance a coy smile. They give each other a hug and Chance turns to the rest of his crew and says, "Everyone, meet Richard Cummings."

"Hi Richard, you old dog, good to see you again and glad to have you aboard." Uncle Miltie says, "You sly devil, Chauncey, why didn't you tell me you had a "mole" inside?"

"That's the way Richard wanted it...for his own safety," Chance replies.

Chance had planted Richard in Charles' confidence when they were still at the other facility, the same way he planted Cora. He poses as a guard and is sent to the compound. The rest of us shake Richard's hand and give him a pat on the back as if to say, we sure are glad you are here. He shows Chance a room where they can put the other guards and they usher them in and lock the door. One of the Guard's gives Richard a shove as he passes by him and mutters under his breath, "Thanks a lot, double-crosser." Richard ignores the comment, as he considers the source. Richard and three of our men go to the Power station and collect the unconscious guards and they are put in the room with the rest of them.

Chip and Trudy stand guard while the rest of us search the area. We find 13 doctors and assistants in the lab area. Chance asks them if there are any others and they motion toward a large door, which is locked. Chance asks Richard for the key and he hands him the key. As he unlocks the door, whom does he find but Dr. Charles Knight on the other side. He is holding a gun with one hand and has the other hand on a lever. Charles pulls the lever down as he holds the gun pointed toward the Glass partition that separates him from us. Chance yells at Richard, "What's that lever for?"

Richard says, "It's the lever to the gas jets that are in the other room where the children are..."

At that instant I run for the door on the far end of the room and bust through and yell, "Charles you filthy, diabolical jerk, how can you kill those children?" I lunge at Charles and he knocks me to the floor with one blow to my head with his gun handle. Just then Chance fires at the glass partition, but it is bullet proof. The room is filled with the latest and best equipment that money can buy. I was out for a while and as I start to wake Charles sits me in a chair and ties me to it. I see Chance and uncle Miltie with their heads together and then Richard walks up to Chance and whispers something in his ear. Chance told me later that when he saw Charles hit me and I hit the floor he went ballistic. Richard grabbed him and calmed him down. Richard knew Chance was about to strangle Charles with his bare hands but he had to subdue him before he did something rash. At this point a level head was most important.

I start to come too and I see the three men move to the right and out of my view. I'm wondering what they are up to. <u>Mercy, my head hurts.</u> Chance is motioning to me; he is shaking his head and drawing his finger across his throat and **with a wink and a nod** I know everything is okay. My head is starting to throb at this point and I'm a little groggy, but I know from his motions that the children are okay. I think to myself, <u>I have to think of a diversion so Chance and the men can get to Charles before he knows what's going on.</u> I start sobbing and Charles yells at me to shut up. I yell back at him, "You ungodly wretch, what have you done?"

Charles says, "Don't worry about what I've done. You should be worrying about what I'm going to do. . .to you."

I sobbed, "I don't care what you do to me. Why did you murder those children?"

Charles says, "They were my property, I can do whatever I want with them."

I answer, "Now I suppose you are going to tell me that you are God Almighty."

His smug comeback is almost enough to make me vomit. He says, "Close, but not quite there yet. Give me a little more time and I will show you who god is."

Just then Miltie, Chance and Richard come bursting through a door to Charles' left and Miltie aims and shoots Charles in his left kneecap. Charles falls to the floor screaming. Miltie says, "Shut up, you insignificant worm. You're lucky I didn't kill you. I just want to see you suffer for a while."

Chance runs over to me and unties me. He says, "I'm so sorry darling, but just after you ran in here, Richard told me he had disconnected the gas to the other chamber a long time ago because he knew something like this would happen. Thanks for that diversion; it gave us a chance to get to another door."

I say, while holding my head, "Diversion, that was no diversion, I wanted to kill Charles. I guess I jumped the gun a little, huh?" Chance got some ice and put it on my head. "Wow that feels good. Thanks honey."

Chance then goes over to check on Charles and puts a tourniquet on his leg and two of the men lift him up and carry him to the infirmary. Chance doctors his knee and puts him on a cot. He gives him some knockout drops in a shot so he won't cause any more trouble for a while, which will give us a chance to look around.

Richard comes over and whispers to Chance, "All this is just the tip-of-the-iceberg; wait until you see what's in his computer."

Chance and I recognized some of the doctors in the other room. We really don't have time for a formal greeting, but when the dust settles, we want to go back and strangle each and every one of them. I've never been as distressed as I am at this moment. We all just stand there and look at

122

each other with utter dismay. We immediately go to the room where the children are being kept.

It is beyond belief what we encounter in that room. Some of the children are in cribs others are in a playpen area and they look to be a few months apart in development. They even look somewhat alike. Cora counted 37 children who reached maturity from their man-made wombs. I had been working on a related project just before I left the lab. My part was to have similar eye color, hair color, and skin tones in the experimental human. I had perfected it just before the "accident". "That slime ball; he got rid of me on purpose," I yell. "He needed my material and he knew I wouldn't go along with his fiendish plans unless he had something on me. That murderer killed my colleagues just so he could frame me; and for what. . .for this?"

Tears start to flow down my face, and Chance grabs me and holds me tight. "I had no idea the magnitude of what Charles and his cohorts have done. I suspected you were framed, but didn't want to believe they would go that far. This proves it. They went to the extreme on this one," Chance tells me. "I am so sorry, Sweetheart."

"I sure am glad Charles didn't have the chance to murder the children," Chance says.

#

Chance explains, "Richard Cummings is one of the men on my team. He never came to Worcester, because he has been at the Bethesda Facility. I brought him into the Lab shortly after I arrived there. The last time I was at the Bethesda lab, I didn't contact Richard." He adds, "There was no need to take the risk of someone asking questions about the two of us being seen talking together. Richard posed as a guard. His credentials are exemplary. He was never introduced to the other men; accept for Miltie, for a good reason. That reason is his covert standing with the N.I.C.A. Miltie and I are the only ones who knew of him, until now. His instructions were to get as close to Charles as he could so Charles would take him with him when ever he left Bethesda for the Wyoming compound. Our plan worked perfect."

#

Richard says, "Dr. Willows, I disconnected those gas jets a long time ago. I knew something like this would happen. Dr. Knight would have killed those kids, you can believe that. I mean, why else would those gas jets be installed if he didn't plan on executing someone, right?"

I answer, "God Bless you."

Chance says, "Thanks Richard, I knew I could count on you." Chance quickly looks around the room and asks, "Is everyone all right? Has anyone checked on the others?"

Not everyone has been accounted for, but the ones at hand seem to be all right. No one has had time to check with the others. Cora says, "Everyone seems to be fine, Chance, except for Laura with that goose egg on her head".

"Has anyone heard from the rest of the team? Where are Wayne and Bobby Joe?" Chance inquires.

"I'll go and check on the others for you Chauncey," Miltie offers.

As I get a closer look at the room, I see that most of the equipment is state-of-the-art. There are machines that I have never even seen before. I ask, "Chance, what are all these machines for anyway?"

Chance looks around and says, "Honey, these machines are the latest in reproductive experiments and cloning experiments."

I am breathless and I gasp, "What in the world is Charles thinking?"

"I don't think I have to tell you what they are for. Dear Old Charles has been experimenting with the embryos we have been sending him. He probably figured he could do better going in another direction."

"That's what I was afraid of." I ask, "Do you think Charles is cloning? Because that's what I think."

"You bettcha, Laura." Chance says in a whisper.

"This place certainly is equipped for anything. There is enough food and medical supplies to last for several years," I observe. "This is only what they have in their larders. There is still tons of food in the gardens and orchards that are yet to be harvested."

Cora says, "They have state-of-the-art equipment and their Medical supplies are comparable to that of a large hospital. Wow, what a place this turned out to be. I shudder to think what this has cost the tax payers."

"They sure took the government for a royal ride on this one," Chance exclaims, as he glances around the room. We are in the area where most of the experiments are taking place. "They have just about every piece of equipment known to the medical world in here. No wonder the government was suspicious of Charles. They just couldn't put everything together without actually seeing everything. That's where I came in." Chance adds.

I say, "Veni, Vidi, Vici."

Milton says, "Right on Laura, *We Came, We Saw, We **kicked ass**.*"

They are growing hybrid varieties of several different vegetables. In the orchards they have apple trees, orange trees, peach, pear and cherry trees. It reminds me of a botanical center. I comment, "I just ate one of the apples I saw on the table in the other room. They are wonderful, or perhaps I'm just hungry."

Richard says, "They can raise everything but livestock because they aren't equipped for them here. Their meat supplies are produced elsewhere, frozen and flown in. There is beef, chicken, lamb and pork in their freezers. All the meat is raised in a sterile environment in New Mexico. I'll give you all the details on that later." Richard takes Chance, Cora and me on a cook's tour of the compound. We are dumbfounded at the sight of this place. My head is really hurting, but I don't let on because I want to see this amazing complex.

Richard takes us into an area where the embryos are kept. It looks like something from a science fiction movie. There are tubular glass vials on shelves against one wall. Each is the size of a two quart bottle. Each vial contains an embryo. They are suspended in a liquid which appears to be similar to the fluids in a woman's womb. The vials are connected to a network of machines and tubes feeding nutrients to the embryos. "There must be hundreds of embryos in here." I say with amazement.

Richard says, "Chauncey, take a look into this room. This is where Dr. Knight keeps all his secrets on his computer."

Chance walks over to the computer platform and knowing a lot about computers breaks the code and gets into Charles' files. Chance says, "I've solved the algorithm to break into Charles' files. Charles is an algomist; he has altered the DNA on all the children."

Chance, along with his many other talents, is a computer nerd. Now, I can handle a Computer when it comes to getting my E-Mail and writing a few letters, however, Chance can build a computer from the ground up. Chance says, "There is another shipment on its way with five more fetuses. It is to arrive in three days. We have to get the bodies buried and everything cleaned up so there will be no suggestion that anything is amiss here."

Richard tells us, "No one ever knew when the shipments were coming in. Charles kept all that information to himself. He didn't want anyone knowing anything other than doing his or her assigned job.

As I look at Richard he looks sort of familiar. I think I remember seeing him at the Experimental Lab. Richard turns and looks at me and says, "Don't you remember me, Doctor? I was the one who used to let you out when you worked late at the lab."

"Now I remember you," I say, "I was so tired when I worked late I could barely see anyone. I'm sure glad you are one of us. You were always so polite and nice."

"Well, thank you Maam. I thought you were very nice also." Richard adds, "By the way, I knew you were set up when those doctors were poisoned, but I couldn't say anything. In fact I didn't even say anything to Chauncey about it. And don't worry, I took those lying statements out of your file and burned them a few days after you left the facility."

"Thanks. I can sure breath easier now that I know that. You are a jewel." I give him a big hug and a pat on the back.

Richard adds, "By the way, those doctors who Charles disposed of were a thorn in his side. He got rid of them on purpose. They weren't in-sync with his way of thinking. I think Charles thought they might turn him in, so he murdered them."

I shake my head and put my arms around him and give him another hug. I am so mentally drained I can hardly function at this point and my head still hurts. Richard feels me trembling and helps me to a chair and sits me down and says, "Now, little lady, you just sit for a spell."

At this point I can't hide the fact that my head is splitting. "Thanks, I think I really need to lie down. Could you please find me some Advil or something for my splitting headache?" Chance has gone into another room and I whispered in Richard's ear, "Don't let Chance see me lying down. He will worry about me and all I need right now is to rest a bit."

"You got it, Maam. I know just where they keep the Advil. You just rest now."

Cora comes over to me and says, "What did you think you were going to accomplish when you rushed into that room where Charles was?"

"I don't know, I don't think I was thinking. I just heard Richard telling Chance about the gas jets and I went nuts."

"How are you feeling now? Are you okay after that whack you took to your head from Charles?"

"I have felt better. Richard just went to get me some Advil for my headache. Don't say anything to Chance. I don't want him worrying about me. He has enough on his plate right now."

"Gotcha. Mums the word."

Chapter XXVIII

UNEXPECTED DISCOVERY

A few hours later I get up and go into the room where Charles keeps his computer. "Oh no," Chance shouted. "Charles has been involved in selling the fetus' organ parts to experiment labs in the U. S., Europe, and Asia. He has been making millions of dollars off this project. Look at these figures, Laura." I walk over and can hardly believe the figures. In one account there is a little more than $200,000,000. There are several similar accounts.

"He sells the organs to experiment labs for the sole purpose of cloning them. These organs are then sold to people, who need a new heart, kidney, liver, lung, etc. These organs carry very big price tags. Most of the cloned organs are sold in the Arab countries. Charles has been selling these parts for several years. He has accumulated enormous bank accounts. It's a good concept, but he is running a 'Black Market' and making a bundle. Wait until the IRS gets a load of this." Chance explains.

I say, "He must be one of the sources we have been reading about."

"I would venture to say he probably started the entire operation. It has grown into a gigantic business," Chance adds.

"That fiend," Cora says. "Chauncey, **please,** let me go in there and kill him, NOW!"

Chance smiles and says, "Oh, don't worry Cora, he will get his soon enough.

I tremble as I speak, "If I had known that Charles was doing this, I would have kicked the stuffing out of him. I certainly did not expect this sort of thing to be going on."

Cora adds, "I don't know about you folks, but I'm getting a little sick to my stomach."

I say, "I'll hold your head if you hold mine while both of us throw up."

Chance says, "Here are all his accounts. He was so sure of himself that he would not be found out; he didn't even try to put anything into a code. He has several Swiss bank accounts; and here are the numbers."

"Chance, are you thinking what I'm thinking?" I ask.

"I think I am." He answers. "Let's get the money out of Charles's Swiss bank accounts and split it among the surviving children. They will be taken care of for the rest of their lives. They will have their school paid for...they will be able to start their own business...they will be very comfortable. They will be able to do whatever they want to do in life. But first, we need to contact the IRS and settle with them. I'm sure there will be plenty money after taxes for the children. I'm sure "Phantom" will approve of splitting the money among the children. But I will check with him on this regardless."

"Great idea, Chance. Is that what you were thinking, Laura?" Asks Cora.

"Right on!" I say. "Go to it Chance. Clean out those accounts. Charles sure won't need that money in prison, because that's where he will be going very soon."

Chance contacts his attorney, Gene McGuire, in Osage, who is handling his trust fund. He asks him to set things up for the children. After explaining everything in detail to Gene, Chance gives him the numbers for the Swiss bank accounts and he takes it from there. "Thanks Gene, I knew I could count on you." Chance says.

We talk about the children and decide to find families to adopt them.

According to Chance's figures, the children will have around $67,000,000 in each account after taxes. He sets it up so that the adoptive parents can use part of the interest to help raise the child they are adopting. Chance says, "Gene says he will see to it that the adoptive parents receive a check every month. With that amount of money in the bank, they can live off some of the interest until they are old enough to handle their own money."

The adoptive parents will be told about the Trust Fund only after they decide to adopt a child or two. That way there is no incentive for them to adopt, other than love for the child.

Chance finds the list of the other abortion clinics that are contributing to the project. He sends a "Cancellation Order, Until Further Notice", to all of them. He signs it, Dr. Charles Knight. He even finds Charles' code name, **Fast Track**. "Give me a break." Chance says with disgust in his voice.

I never questioned my orders from Charles, so we were hoping the other clinics wouldn't question this one. We never hear back from any of them, so we conclude that they have followed the order.

The shipment of the five fetuses is already in the process of being sent, so there is no way to stop that. Once the fetuses are prepared for shipment, they are frozen and sealed. When they arrive at the compound, they are thawed and injected with a serum that revives them. The fetuses are placed into the makeshift womb, nurtured, and left there to mature.

Richard tells Chance where their meat supply is processed, "It's on an area outside of Albuquerque, on some government owned land between Gonzales Ranch and White Lakes."

Chance notifies "Phantom" to go in and shut it down. Chance says, "Charles must have told them they were doing this for the government. That way they wouldn't question anything."

Chance has a long discussion with "Phantom". He tells him about everything that has occurred up to now. "Phantom" approved of everything Chance has done and tells him to handle everything to his own discretion. "Phantom" apologizes to Chance for this horrible situation that he has to clean up.

My next task is to attend to the progression of the fetuses that are not yet developed to maturity. Cora is acquainted with some of the procedure in the experiment, so she and I put our heads together and try to figure out what to do next. There are 180 more embryos that are not completely developed and they are kept in their incubator type containers. The rest of the containers are ready and waiting for the next arrival of the frozen embryos. Cora and I fret over the fate of the embryos for several hours.

We talk it over with everyone on the team and we all concur that we should turn off the machines that are keeping the embryos alive. It just seems more humane to all of us.

I choose to go one step further and look at the embryos under the microscope and my suspicions are correct. "Come look at this, Cora."

Cora looks into the lens. "These fetuses are missing some of their organs."

I said, "Exactly! This must be Charles' incubator for the organs that he has been selling. He isn't developing the children, he's developing the organs. We made the right decision didn't we?"

Chance says, "It looks to me like Charles put a hold on his 'Perfect Society', and decided to make some big cash on the side. He expanded his business."

I say, "This must be why Charles wanted us to 'not be so fussy' in the selections we were sending him. He apparently abandoned his Perfect Society and decided to go with just the organs instead."

Cora says, "I'll bet that's exactly what happened. He gave up on the children, and instead, in his greed, wanted to make a profit with the organs."

I add, "That's why he was willing to gas the children. He knew he could do better, money-wise, with the fetal organs. Playing god was put on the shelf apparently."

"It looks like we got here just in time, Chance," Cora says.

"We sure did, Cora, and I'm wondering if perhaps Charles was experimenting with cloning long before any of us even gave it a thought. It never even entered my mind that he would be into this." He says.

"At this point," I say, "I wouldn't put anything passed Charles."

We are all completely aghast at what has been taking place here. Milton says, "I have been reading about the 'fetal organs' that are being sold for millions of dollars to experimental labs to be used for cloning purposes, and also are being sold to the Multi-rich for new cloned organs. I never even fathomed that this place would be into that. We all had our minds set on the "Perfect Society". It never entered my mind that Charles would be doing this."

"I wonder if this is the only place these 'fetal organs' are being harvested." Cora says.

"I hope it is," Chance says, "Or we are in for another Raid very soon."

"Boy, wait 'til "Phantom" hears about this," Cora says. "Or do you think he might already know?" She adds, "Chauncey, *pleeeze*, let me go in there and strangle Charles." Chance almost lets her have at him.

"I hope "Phantom" doesn't know about this new development." Chance says, "I'm going to be one ticked-off dude, if he does and he didn't tell me about it." Chance adds, with a smirk, "and **no**, you cannot go in there and strangle Charles, as much as I would like to do it myself, we have to let the courts take care of him. Whoa, look at this, there are a few names in here that would indicate that a lot of the organs were bought by Arabs."

#

"Phantom" never interferes with Chance when he makes his plans for any of the covert assignments that he and the team are on. Chance contacts him often and keeps him abreast of their plans, but Chance is always in charge. When there is a big decision to be made and Chance is having difficulty with how to perform the right solution, he will contact "Phantom" and they will discuss the problem. Chance figures everything out himself, most of the time, but it's nice to have someone to use as a sounding board. Chance says, "I've never met "Phantom" and he has never met me. We are completely anonymous to each other. We are just voices over the phone. And it's best to keep it that way. He knows my record and everything about me. I know nothing about him. In the past we have communicated through messages or phone only."

Chapter XXIX

PONDERING OUR NEXT STEP

We are now left with another problem at hand. What do we do with this facility after we leave? We know we can't just leave all this food to go to waste. Chance is torn between destroying the entire complex or keeping it as it is and coming up with an idea for its use. We can't take the chance of someone coming upon this site and finding all this. "What a waste," I said. "It is too bad we can't find a way to use this facility for something good instead of for why it was built."

Chance says, "I'm just glad that a potential human disaster has been thwarted."

"Amen to that," I say.

We turn to Hank, Billy, Richard, and a few others who come up with a plan of destruction for the entire area without the whole world knowing about it.

Richard shows us a Bulldozer and other earth-moving equipment that the Compound used for building all this. They will need the heavy equipment to aid them in the destruction. There is a man-made Lake at the site. Hank comes up with the idea to bulldoze everything into the lake. No one will ever be using that lake, so they agree that it is an excellent idea to get rid of all the evidence of anything other than a mountain wilderness existed here.

The rest of us harvest the food supply and put it in the many baskets we find, and have the helicopters come to pick it up. What the lodge can't use, we are sure the Homeless Shelters can. Chance and I are firm believers of the old adage, "Waste Not, Want Not". There are shipping boxes that the meat is put into and taken immediately to the lodge. Joanne is quite skilled in the kitchen at conserving.

The meat is put into the immense freezers at the Lodge. Joanne cans the fruits and vegetables for later use. When we returned to the Lodge, we all pitch in and helped with the canning. We pick all the ripe fruit and pack it into boxes. We have the doctors and guards help with the food. There is just too much to do in such a short time. Chance pulls up all the records on the computer and we have to log all the living children's records onto a floppy disk for later utilization. Chance, Wayne and Uncle Miltie bury the dead guards very deep.

When we are finished with everything we need off Charles' computer, Chance destroys its contents and the machine so that no one can ever break into the information that it contained.

Wayne comes to Chance and says, "Chauncey, Can I talk to you for a minute?"

Chance says, "Sure Wayne, what is it. You look so serious."

Wayne says, "Well, I've been thinking about what you all have been talking about. . .destroying all of this and it hurts me to think that we can't find another way for a better use of this place. It's so perfect here. You have no climate to worry about, no food to worry about. This entire place is self-sufficient. Think about it Chauncey, what if we could turn this place into something like a camp for orphans or a youth camp of some sort. We could get rid of the guns and all that stuff. The lake could be used for teaching the kids how to canoe and how to swim. They could learn how to farm the crops and the orchards. It would be a perfect place for children. What do you think?"

Chance yells, "Hey everyone, come here, Wayne has just had an epiphany. I think he has an excellent idea. I think we should give this some consideration. Go ahead, Wayne, tell them your idea."

Wayne explains everything he just told Chance and all of us cheer and Miltie says, "What a terrific idea. Do you think we could pull it off Chauncey?"

Chance says, "Let me bounce this idea off "Phantom" and see what he thinks. After all the government has paid for all this, and I think it's a super idea. Your idea certainly won't need all this medical equipment but I'm sure we can find some solution for its use. I'll go call him now. Thanks, Wayne, you're a genius."

I walk over to Wayne and give him a big hug and kiss on the cheek and say, "Wayne, you have just made this entire mission a complete and utter success."

He turns beet red and says, "Thanks Laura, that sure means a lot to me."

Wayne says, "Well, all you guys are so darn busy with everything else, I figured your heads were just too full of other stuff. You would have come up with this same solution when you had time to think about it. I'm just sure you would have."

Chapter XXX

SAVING TRUDY

#

    Chip Dagget and his wife, Trudy, are injured very badly when one of the guards gets loose. The guard uses a key hidden in his boot to unlock the door. He has a knife concealed in his boot also and uses the weapon on Trudy and Chip. We didn't think to strip search these guys. We put Chip and Trudy in the infirmary and Cora, the other women and I are attending to them. Bobby Joe Caldwell is shot when he enters the Dome. There is a guard we don't see on top of a hilly area.

    Just as the big doors are blown he catches Bobby Joe in his sights and puts a bullet in him. He too, is put in the infirmary. We certainly have our hands full with the wounded. We have all the medical tools we need to care for their injuries. No one's wounds are too serious except for Trudy's. Chance calls the lodge and asks Mickey to get back here as soon as he has Willie stabilized. He tells Mickey about Trudy and he is back here in two hours.

    Chance and I are working on Trudy to stop the bleeding, and we try to determine how severe her wounds really are. We conclude she will need a specialist and further surgery. I said, "Chance, it looks like the guard severed her spinal cord. What do you think?"

    Chance checked very closely and said, "I don't think it's severed all the way, but it's close to it."

    We check periodically with the lodge to see how Willie is doing and he is just fine. He won't be using his left arm for a while, though. The guard got him in the left shoulder. The guard, who went back with Willie, has died.

#

The men start cleaning up as much as they can, so everything looks normal. When the helicopter comes with the new embryos, Chance and Richard meet him at the Heliport outside the dome and accept the container. They try to act nonchalant. The pilot mutters something about, "Where's the Doc?"

Chance tells him he is busy with an experiment. The pilot says he is supposed to ask for a pass word when the Doc isn't here. Chance says, "Fast Track". The pilot never asks another question, gets into his helicopter and flies away. Chance says, "Phew that was close."

Richard asks, "How did you come up with that pass word?"

"That is Charles' code name. I figured he would use it as a pass word also. I'm sure glad I was right or we would have another prisoner on our hands."

Chance deems the pilot isn't aware of what is in the containers, so there is no reason to detain him. We had already discussed what we would do with the new embryos when they arrived. Everyone agreed that it would be wise not to go through the thawing process of reviving this new package of frozen embryos. What would be the sense in that? Chance disposed of the package as humanely as he could.

#

The entire complex's large weaponry is destroyed. Eight of the guards are killed in the explosion; 11 are captured; however, the one guard who attacked Chip and Trudy was also killed; so that makes nine guards dead and ten captured. Hank comes around the corner just in time to save Chip, who is struggling with the guard. Hank shoots the guard just as the guard raises his knife to stab Chip in the heart. Hank checks Chip and quickly turns to look at Trudy, who is on the floor bleeding and losing consciousness. Hank lifts her up like she is a delicate china doll and cradles her in his strong arms. He yells at one of the other men to help with Chip. At this point they meet up with Richard who shows them the way to the infirmary; and Hank carries Trudy to the infirmary and places her gently on one of the beds. Chip is badly slashed on his arm and chest. Chance, Cora and I start first aid immediately on both of them.

Bobby Joe is shot in the thigh. He goes down with a thud. Wayne grabs him and pulls him out of the way. He takes aim and kills the guard who shot Bobby Joe. Wayne tears his shirt and ties it around Bobby Joe's leg, until he can get some medical help for him. When it is all over, Wayne helps Bobby Joe as he limps to the infirmary. Chance gets the bullet out of Bobby Joe's leg and sews him up. He is a little sore, but he will be all right.

Chapter XXXI

MEETING THE CHILDREN

Finally we enter the "Gas Chamber" where the children are being kept. They all look quite similar, yet they each have their own distinctive look. Cora says, "Let's get them out of this room; it's making me sick just thinking about what could have happened to them in here. It is a little exhausting trying to tell them apart. I notice that none of the children has African-American features, so I have to believe that either my experiment worked or the fetus that I sent them from the young girl with the black boyfriend didn't survive, or perhaps it is still in the incubators with the other fetuses. We take all the children into a friendlier environment. There is a room that looks like it was meant for a party or entertainment room. There are chairs, tables, TVs and even some desks in this room. "Perhaps this is where the children are schooled," I whisper to Chance.

Chance takes a shine to one child who is off by himself. He seems to be one of the more mature children. Chance goes over to him, smiles and holds out his hand for the child to take. The boy looks up at Chance and tries to smile as he puts his tiny hand into Chance's. He is aping Chance.

"I don't think these children know how to smile. He seems to be mocking you." I observe.

"I think you're right, darling," Chance replies.

"What is smile?" The child says.

"My word," Chance says, "You can talk?"

"I can talk, I can read, I can think." The child replies.

I turn to the boy and ask, "What is your name, sweetheart?"

His reply took everyone completely by surprise. "I am number 2-2-4," he answers.

The children are numbered rather than named. This really enrages everyone. "Those sanctimonious nerds. They can't even take the time to name the children. They are just numbers to them." I say in a whisper. "I'm sorry Chance, but I just can't be magnanimous when it comes to Charles, I wish he was dead.

Cora says, "Don't beat yourself up too much, Laura, I feel the same as you, I never did like him. I always thought he was an arrogant jerk."

Chance says, "Speaking of Charles has anyone checked on him lately? We've all been so busy, I almost forgot about him."

Richard says, "I'll check on him for you Chauncey, where did you put him?"

Chance answers, "He's in the other room. It looks like an infirmary. I put him in one of the beds in there, away from the others."

Everyone starts giving the children names. Cora says, "This one looks like an Angel, I'm naming her Angela. Cora wonders out loud, "Just what did these Scientists really have in store for these children?"

"Good question, but I think we are better off not knowing the answer to that one." I reply.

I think the children are not much over 22 months old, some a little younger, but the older ones would be at a speaking age but not like this child. He is almost robotic. It seems he has progressed to at least a four year old. "I think he might be a genius." Chance says.

"Do you suppose they did something to their minds to make them brilliant?" I ask.

Chance scratches his head and answers, "I think someone at the Center worked on something like that but I never really thought they had any luck. At least they didn't announce it to the rest of us if they did; besides, I was working on a completely different project at that time." Chance recalls.

We all come to the conclusion that this facility has been here a lot longer than we first thought. "They had to have had this compound built at least four years ago," Chance says. "It would have taken at least three years to build this facility. They have everything here. We could stay here for a long time and be very comfortable, with all the modern conveniences that are here."

Chance says, "I wonder where they were getting their supply of fetuses before they contacted me. The CIA planted me into the project about four years before you came in, Laura. At that time no one confided in me as to any of the goings-on at the project, other than the normal day to day experiments. I was under the impression that they were in the beginning stages of the program. It wasn't until much later that they brought me into their confidence." Chance recalled that Charles would have long talks with him on several occasions. He said, "Charles was probably on a 'fishing expedition' to see if he could trust me." Chance played right into his hands and eventually Charles accepted him.

Mentally, these children are progressed way beyond their young ages. They have the bodies of infants to toddlers and the minds of three, four and five year olds. We discovered that the little boy Chance befriends is a natural genius. The children are all very intelligent but he is more intelligent than the rest who are around his age. Chance names him Donald, and we call him Donny. Chance says, "I had a very dear friend with whom I grew up, named Donald Sharp. We were best friends all through grade school. One day Donald's family moved to Europe and I never heard from him again. I was very sad for a few years after that, because I missed my friend. I never forgot Donald and often wondered what happened to him. I hope he is alive and happy."

As we become more acquainted with the children, we become increasingly attached to them. Chance and I make arrangement to adopt Donald. Several of the men and their wives choose names for the children from friends or relatives whom they admire. And yes, they adopt these children also. Cora adopts Angela. We thought she was about nine or ten months old.

Chance, Cora and I are the only ones on our team who know about the money these children will receive. We are the only ones who know about the arrangements that are made for the children. No one is told about their inheritance until after the adoptions are final. Not that Chance or I thought any of them would adopt out of greed, but we just thought it best not to say anything to anyone until the proper time. Some of our friends, whom we trust, take several of the children as their own. Jake and Fran Winters, love children but can't have any of their own, so they adopt three of the younger ones. Chance says that the younger children will never remember any of this and it will be easier for them to live a normal life. The fact that the three children, Jake and Fran adopt, look so much alike, they are able to pass them off as triplets and adopt them as such. Because of the altered DNA of these children, no one will know that they are not natural siblings. For that very reason, we never allow the children to see one another after they are adopted. Their identities are forever kept clandestine.

Jake turns to Fran, with one of the babies in his arms and says, "Looks like our dancing days are over for a while, honey."

Fran comes back, "Oh no you don't . . . we are still going dancing on Saturday nights. You don't want to deprive all the people who are counting on us to entertain them do you?" We all have a good chuckle.

Most of the children are in the younger stages. There are only five who are in the older group. I wonder perhaps if the older group had probably started their lives at the Center, before this place was built. We will never know exactly when or where this misfortune was started. Chance says, "I'm sure we will never get the truth out of Charles."

The information that Chance finds on the children in the computers is in code and practically impossible to break. He has figured out some of it, but it is just taking too long and we have more important things to conquer. Besides, all the information in the computer is going to be destroyed. We have to make up new records for the children.

Out of the 35 children, our team adopts 12 of them. So now, we only need to find families to adopt 23 children. The agreement is, however, that once the children are placed in families, they are never to see each other again. We don't want to have to explain their similarities to them or anyone. Therefore, we can only let one set of parents adopt a child; no one else in that family will be allowed to adopt any of the children. The children also are never to know about their beginnings or that they are adopted. The children never need to know that they were the products of "Eugenics" experiments by the evil Dr. Charles Knight and his cronies.

As we are fussing over the children, Richard comes running into the room. He motions to Chance and whispers something into his ear. He and Chance leave the room. Several minutes go by and I am getting very curious. Soon Chance comes back into the room and asks us to leave the children for a moment because he needs to talk to us. We go out into another room and Chance tells us that Charles has committed suicide. He had somehow gotten hold of a cyanide tablet. Richard found him lying on the floor with foam flowing from his mouth.

"Whenever I think of Charles, which isn't very often, I think of him as Hitler reincarnated. I sure hope and pray there aren't any more like him out there." I say.

Chance says, "I'm sure there will be another "Charles" some day. Let's just pray we can stop him too. People like Charles are too much of a coward to face the punishment that was due him. It doesn't surprise me at all that he killed himself. He probably had the cyanide pill on him. I didn't think to search him."

Chapter XXXII

THE ADOPTION PROCESS

    Chance knows of an adoption agency in Iowa and he contacts them to see if there might be someone looking for a child who has not been able to be placed with one. They have several. Because of the strict laws that govern adoption in this country, many people, who would be great parents, don't get coupled with the adoptable children for one reason or another. Chance is able to cut through all the Red Tape and he finds several families through his contacts.

    The adoptive parents receive a bankbook for each child that they adopt. Chance tells them that the money is for the child; however, they are to use the interest from the money, as they need it in raising them. The bulk of the money in each account is put in a trust fund for each child and it is not to be touched until that child turns 21 years old. Most of the families who adopt the children are not strapped for money, so they let the interest build in the trust funds and only take out what is needed for their schooling or other essentials.

    Chance has put himself and me as Executors of the Trust Fund. We will see that each child receives his or her money when they come of age. "Phantom" tells Chance to go ahead and divide the money. He says, "It isn't the Governments money per se, and it should belong to the children. Whatever taxes Dr. Wright owes will come off the top." Chance and I, however, exempt ourselves from using any of this money, as Chance says he has enough of his own to make Donny comfortable for the rest of his life.

    Chance has friends in the right places and there will be no problem with all the paper work for these people to adopt the children. Everything will be legal and above board, however, there will be no way to ever trace their births, or their birth parents. All the records are kept as though the children are "Test Tube" babies from what Chance can deduce from the files. The computers are destroyed once we obtain the information we need from them. This, in turn, destroys all records of the children and their existence. New birth certificates are made for each child to show that the adoptive parents are their natural birth parents.

Cora and I run blood tests on all the children. We are bowled over at the results of our tests. The children are **disease free** and will never have in-born disorders, such as MD, MS, Cystic Fibroses, polio etc. etc. The scientists were able to completely change the "Gene" structure of the fetuses and they will never have any childhood or inherited diseases such as heart disease, cancer, diabetes, etc. They have the purest blood in the world.

If nothing else, Charles at least did something right in giving these children such pure blood. All this will be explained to the new parents and will never be revealed to the children. All the adoptive parents agree to act as if the children are their own and not adopted. It is all very complicated, yet very simple. They will just act as though the children were born to them. Chance sees to it that all the adoptive families are screened thoroughly before they are allowed to become parents of these children. These children are very precious and special and the families need to know how important it is that they follow the rules of the adoptions. We try to get as close as we can to make up birth dates for all of them. It isn't difficult to place them in good families. There are so many wonderful couples who desperately want and love children. What they, the Scientist who were involved in all this, didn't know is that the children are all **sterile**.

Perhaps Dr. Charles Knight would turn over in his grave if he knew that his experiment backfired. His perfect little society isn't so perfect after all. The children find out they are sterile after they reach adulthood, marry and want to start families of their own. Some of them adopt children and are very happy with their families; never knowing that they too are adopted. Chance and I have always kept in contact with the parents of all the children. We receive yearly reports of their progress which are properly burned after they are read.

"Chance," I ask, with a quizzical look, "Do you suppose Charles did know that the children were sterile and that's why he started selling the fetal organs? After all he had an endless supply of parts. And that would explain why he was willing to kill the children."

"We will never know the answer to that, Laura, but it would make sense as to why he was willing to execute the children," Chance says.

"I was just sort of thinking out loud," I say.

"I think it is rather ironic, that those other scientist went to all that trouble of trying to make a 'perfect society' and it would have all ended because of the sterility of their subjects." Cora says.

"The idea of a "Pure" race is not a bad one," I said. "By pure, I mean free from any and all diseases or maladies. Wouldn't it be nice to be assured that every birth would produce a healthy and perfect child? That would be playing God, in my estimation; and to expect everyone to be perfect is unrealistic."

#

When the time comes to depart this place, instead of leaving the same way we came in, we call for the helicopters to pick us up; plus we have the children to consider. It takes about 10 trips to get all of the children and us back to the lodge. We gather up the rest of the food, that we didn't eat, and take it with us. Several of us take turns preparing our meals. That's a lot of cooking for all of the children, the prisoners and us. The doctors and their assistants, whom we captured, are sent to a Federal Prison along with the nine guards. No tears are shed over the likes of that bunch.

Clyde Kenner tried to talk his way out of a prison term by offering to tell us anything we wanted to know. Chance told him, "I already know everything I want to know about your operation." Madelyn Shultz just sat there and sneered at us. Homer Van Elsten was in tears and pleading for mercy. Chance told them they all came into this with their eyes wide open and what ever they get, they deserve.

#

Chance and I sometimes talk about the doctors from the lab, and cannot figure out why they would go along with Charles on all this nonsense. We knew all of them and always thought they were decent doctors and very intelligent people. "Perhaps Charles had something on **them** also," Chance says.

"Well, if he could do it to me, I guess he could do it to anyone." Because of the sensitivity of the subject matter of the project, "Phantom" saw to it that the scientists and guards would never be released from prison. They are isolated from the other prisoners and they have no communication with the outside world. It is as if they vanished off the face of the earth. Most of them had no families. The ones, who did have family, lost all contact with their relatives' years ago because they wanted it that way. Chance says, "I think Charles not only had something on these people, he also picked people who had no family ties. That even included all the guards. Everyone was single and had no family on the outside. Charles thought of everything."

"The last I heard, there aren't too many of them left. They have either died, or too senile to remember anything." I say.

Chance tells the adoptive parents of the children's beginnings and they are sworn to secrecy. We all know how important this situation is and no one has ever spoken of the things that took place here. I am revealing it now because many of the people involved have passed on. The children are all grown and have families of their own; and no one is the wiser about their beginnings. I have changed all the names and places in case someone should come across this journal and wonder if all this is true or not.

Chance says, "The less we think about them, the better we will feel. "I sure hope the new teams of young men are as devoted to this country as we are."

"Amen again darling," I add.

Chapter XXXIII

THE FINALE

Bobby Joe, Hank, and the two brothers, Ken and Freddy Zimmerman, along with Richard, stay after the rest of us leave for the lodge and finish getting rid of all evidence of the destroyed canon and guns. Chance got the word from "Phantom" that the camp for children was a wonderful idea and they could go ahead and make their plans. Wayne volunteers to oversee the operation of converting everything to make it into a Youth Camp. Before he did that, however, he had to go back to his place and take care of a few things first. Chance and I were pleased with this new arrangement. Wayne was able to sell his property to one of his pilot friends who lost his home in a fire. He was thrilled to get it. "Phantom" was pleased with the idea of a youth camp and told us to take what was not needed for the camp and put it to good use. "Use your own discretion," he tells Chance.

Most of the men stay at the compound for about three weeks. It takes that long to get everything set up for the new camp, and to prepare the children for their new lives. Wayne knows several pilots at the airport in Riverton, and they offer to help bring everyone out. They all have their own helicopters. Most of them are ex-military. They are also Wayne's trusted friends and know the importance of keeping everything covert.

Willie recovers nicely and is mad that he missed all the action. He doesn't complain about the excellent care he receives from Joanne, however. She waits on him hand and foot.

Hank's wife, Rene, joins him at the lodge. Hank calls and tells her about the children and she catches the first flight she can get. They adopt a little girl.

We see our first snowfall of the season while we are at the Lodge. "What a beautiful place this is," I said.

"We will have to come back some time and go skiing, Laura," Chance says.

"Not I," I say. "You won't see me on skis. I will sit and enjoy the scenery and breathe in that wonderful fresh air while you are out there breaking a limb."

Chance teases me and says, "You big baby, I'll get you on a pair of skis and you will love it."

Chip and Bobby Joe are recovering nicely; however, Trudy will need some therapy. A nerve is severed in her neck and surgery is done to repair the area and to try to re-connect the nerve. We did as much as we could at the compound but she needs extensive surgery. She is flown to Johns Hopkins Hospital where they can better take care of her needs until she recovers. We are all anxious until word comes that everything has gone well and she will be back on her feet in a matter of weeks. A sigh of relief can be heard throughout the team as we get the good news. Someone in the group yells, "Praise God." I think we all said a little prayer of thanks at that moment. At least I know I did.

Chance quit the Science Lab position. Well, he didn't actually quit; once we re-constructed the compound in Wyoming, the government replaced everyone at the Biomedical Lab and started new projects that wouldn't create so much controversy. "Phantom" elected to drop all those experiments and destroy all the records. This action also destroys any trace of my fabricated "Mishap", just in case Richard didn't get all of it. I no longer have to worry about being blackmailed ever again.

I was glad they did keep the embryonic stem cell research in operation. It is so important for the betterment of mankind. The children are all grown and have families of their own; and no one is the wiser about their beginnings. I have changed all the names and places in case someone should come across this journal.

A lot of heads rolled before the dust settled on that project. Chance and his team are still on the N.I.C.A.'s payroll, but they are free to live their lives normally. The government knows that if they ever need them, they will be there. Cora, Mary Jean and I gave our notice at the abortion clinic and a few months later it was closed. We were all glad to see that happen.

I delivered Martha's daughter and she is now living with her parents and working part time at a hospital. Eventually she wants to go to nurse's school and become a Registered Nurse.

For Chance and me, we are very pleased with little Donny. We go on to have two more children of our own...twins, Colette and Kathleen. They are the sweetest little girls you could ever want. The three children get along beautifully, and no one knows that Donny isn't the girl's natural brother. We have treated Donny as if he is our natural child. He is, however, extremely bright. Actually, the girls are quite intelligent as well. Because of the attention we give to Donny, he seems to have no memory of his earlier life at the Compound.

Chance and I have our own private practice in a Medical Clinic, and we are very happy with our family and our Clinic.

We had permission to gather the medical supplies from the compound and take most of the medical machines with us. One of Wayne's friends has a large cargo plane and we used that to transport the state-of-the-art equipment back to Worcester. All of this equipment is very beneficial to us when Chance and I open our Clinic. This is the only way we are able to outfit the clinic. We are ready for anything. We left behind what the Youth Camp will need for an infirmary.

All of this is cleared, however, through "Phantom". He has the final word on everything, especially when it comes to all that expensive equipment. We are not going to take any chance that we will be accused of stealing. In fact, "Phantom" is the one who suggests we take the machinery and other supplies and open our own clinic. He says, "everything has been paid for by the government, and there is no need to waste any of it. The taxes the government will received from Charles' ill gotten gains will be plenty of pay back for his thievery. There is enough waste when it comes to the government." After discussing it with the others, we all agree that it makes more sense than destroying everything.

Chance and I make a pact with the members of the team. We tell them that if they ever need any medical care or treatment they are to come to us and everything will be free. They all agree to take us up on our offer.

Milton says, "Chance, you and Laura can be my doctors any time. I trust you both with my life and the life of my family."

"That goes both ways, Milton," I say, as I walk over to him and give him a big hug and a kiss on the cheek.

Everyone gets in on the act and we all give each other a hug and a kiss on the cheek.

#

After Chance and I bring Rose back into Wayne's life they both decide they would love to run the Camp at the Compound in the mountains. They hire a crew that will help them make the camp a success and off they go.

Wayne didn't adopt any of the children because he figured he will have enough children when the camp opens.

Mary Jean and Cora work with us at the health clinic. And Mary Jean has her children there also. We explain everything to Mary Jean about what we have been up to. She agrees that it is important to keep everything very much to ourselves. Both Cora and I are so happy that Mary Jean has joined us at the clinic. We are the "Three Musketeers" once again.

Chance builds a school-room/play-room in the back of the medical clinic. We hire an educator, who home-schools the children under our supervision. All of our employees bring their children to work with them. Mary Jeans' older children help supervise the younger children. We all take turns seeing that the children are learning and playing with each other in a normal and healthy atmosphere. I took it upon myself, with Chance's permission, to lend Martha the money she needs to go to nursing school. She was very grateful and works for free part time at the clinic. This is her way of paying us back for our help. She brings her baby with her when she comes to the clinic. She had a beautiful baby girl and she named her Laura.

Chance drew up the plans for the clinic, hired a local building contractor and helped in the construction of the building.

Cora turned her adopted child, Angela, over to one of her sisters. When we decided that we didn't want the children to see each other, it was the best solution we could come up with. Her sister is the legal guardian of Angela, but Cora will always be considered her mother. When she gets older, they explain to the child that her mother travels a lot so that is why her aunt is raising her. Sometimes a little white lie is necessary. Angela grows up to be a very fine young lady. Cora's chest puffs out whenever she talks about her. She keeps us informed of her progress. Cora drives to see Angela every weekend while she is growing into an adult. This gives Cora good quality time with her. Her sister lives in the next state and it only takes two hours to drive there and back to Worcester. Cora takes Friday afternoons off so she can spend a little extra time with Angela. We told her to come in on Monday afternoons so she doesn't have to rush and drive at night to get back to Worcester.

Any and all patients are welcome at the clinic, whether they have insurance or not. It is a sort of payback for the free equipment. If they can't pay, Chance and I don't care; we cure them and send them on their way. We don't concern ourselves with HMOs and the like. If they have insurance we honor it. Some of them choose to pay cash.

Many of our patients end up doing work for us in lieu of payment. Harry Clemons, for instance, had some bothersome warts that Chance took care of. We needed bookshelves in the school library so Harry built them for us. All in all it is a very good life for everyone.

Sort of like in the old days when a man pays the doctor in eggs, or a dressed chicken, if he raises chickens; a ham, or some bacon, if he raises pigs; carpentry work for the doctor, if he is a carpenter; a meal, if she is a good cook. 'You do something for me and I do something for you.' 'You give me something and I give you something.' It is called the BARTER System. Too bad money is so important now. It was a less complicated way to live back then.

Every six months or so, our group gets together. We meet in those same woods and have a picnic. We met one time in December. It was quite cold, so we decided to have a wiener roast. We built a small fire and had hot dogs, hot chocolate and toasted marshmallows. We almost burned down the woods. Fortunately, someone had the foresight to bring a large container of water.

Chance says, "I guess we won't try this again."

Chance and I miss our friends a lot, and we will love them all forever. A few people from the team decide to move to Worcester and raise their families. These couples didn't adopt any of the children from the compound, as they already had children of their own. Several couples have five or six kids and they think that is enough.

Once a year we all show up at the Lodge for a reunion. The children are never brought together. I am in contact with all the adoptive parents and they send me pictures every now and then, which is nice for the others to see. We compare notes about the kids, share pictures, and have a few drinks, a few laughs and lots of that great comfort food. We remember our friends who have passed on and are gone from us forever. We mention their names often and hope they are in a happier place.

No matter what, we will always miss the ones who are no longer with us. No one really knows what is beyond our world, we can only speculate. By thinking that our loved ones are in a better place, without pain or heartache, and they are with the ones who have passed before them, it is easier for us who are left behind to justify their leaving us. We hope and pray that all is well on the other side.

Steve and Joanne close the lodge to tourists so we can enjoy each other's company without interruptions. We usually meet during their off season, so it isn't an imposition to them, or their patrons to close for a few days to tourists.

We keep in touch and never speak of the raid in Wyoming. That chapter of our lives is sealed forever in our minds. Chance and his team have a few more problems to conquer and we look back over the years we have spent together and reflect about the many tragedies that were prevented by Chance and his magnificent team of comrades. We all have one regret, however, and that was on September 11, 2001, the destruction of the World Trade Center in New York, the Pentagon Building in Washington DC, the downed plane in Pennsylvania and the murder of thousands of people.

The CIA had hints that something was going to happen but no one knew when or where anything would occur. They could have cracked down on the security at the Air Ports, but before they could get something in operation it was too late. Chance and his team were alerted but before he could put anything into working mode, all hell broke loose and there was no way anyone could have foreseen or prevented that horrible catastrophe. We think about all those people in those buildings and the airplane that crashed in Pennsylvania, and we always take a silent moment to pray for them and their families.

Chance says, "It is suspect that other explosions occurred in the North Tower after the airplane struck. Perhaps the terrorists were able to place bombs in other parts of the building, before it was decided to use airplanes, to make sure the building went down. In all the news reels, it looked like an implosion took place. All in all I believe we were defeated before we even started. This was planned for a long time and we may never know who all is involved and we may never know what really happened. There are too many unanswered questions."

Chance and his unit, made a few more covert trips and raids and many heart-breaking moments had to be overcome. Eventually the team was replaced with a younger group of men who were just as strong, just as brave and just as capable as Chance and the others.

We never did get around to opening our Restaurant. We sure could have, with Chance's knowledge and expertise about food. It's okay though; we still enjoyed great meals with our friends. We have a great kitchen at the clinic and we usually cook lunch for the workers, children and even some of the patients. Chance loves cooking for everyone.

Over the years of our get-togethers, we always marvel at how the children, who are now adults, still look so much alike. We look at one another, and **with a wink and a nod,** we know each other's thoughts, without speaking another word.

#

Back on our cozy sofa Chance and I ponder the past as we relax in the comfort of our home that Chance built many years ago. Our hair has turned to silver and Chance looks sophisticated with his beautiful white hair. He still has most of it. I just look old with my salt and pepper hair.

We have more wrinkles than we did when we started all this, but Chance says we have earned every one of them.

Before Donny married, he did an eight-year stint in the Army. He was stationed at Fort Lee, Virginia.

"You know Chance," I say, "I think we have found our Nirvana right here in our little home and our little Clinic. I have never needed anything else."

"Nor have I, darling," Chance whispers, "So long as you are with me. . .nor have I."

"I think of all the covert operations we have been on for the N.I.C.A., and I think the first one was the most important of any of the others. That's where we reunited and that's where I met your wonderful friends and that's where we found Donny. He is such a blessing in our lives."

"He sure is, honey, I agree that was a wonderful memory so far as reuniting with you and finding Donny, but I think the best one was the last one we were on, because it was the **last one**."

"Good point. Now we are close to the final stage in our lives. We are both a little greyer a few more lines seem to be drawn on my face every time I look in the mirror, but I think I have earned every one of them."

"Lines or no lines, you are more beautiful to me each and every day. I love your little lines." Chance says with pride as he draws his finger back and forth, lightly across my face.

"And here we are, ready to take on one more slice of life that is being dealt to us. . .one more task. . .one more day. Our faces have changed but our goals have stayed the same. We have accomplished much and I hope we have time to accomplish more. Let's see what tomorrow brings." Chance says with pride in his voice.

As we cuddle into each other's arms and reflect on our lives together we know it has been a great life for us both and a very blessed one as we remember all our friends, who are no longer with us. Chance and I are thinking of retiring from the clinic and turning it over to the children. I say, "We have paid our dues to society and I think it's time to turn it over to Donny, Colette and Kathleen." They all went into the medical field and they love working at the clinic and helping others. They will carry on the tradition of giving aid to everyone who walks through the doors, whether they can pay or not. Chance glances up at me and **with wink and a nod** not another word needs to be spoken.

THE END

Author's Note

This story and all the characters are from my imagination. All Cities in this story are real but the situations are made up for the sake of places of origin for my characters. Any indication to anyone you may know is purely coincidental. As for any and all government activities, you can make up your own mind as to which are real and which are not real. If I hit a few truths it was purely by accident.

I have several people I would like to thank for their contribution to the success of my Novel. They are as follows: Cousins Kathleen Finnegan and Colette Wallace (May she rest in Peace) for their encouragement and editing of my first draft. My wonderful husband, Spero, who read, re-read and re-re-read my manuscript until he was sick of it. To my friend, Judy Wahlberg, who encouraged me to continue writing. (God rest her soul.) To my friend the "Story Teller", Mike Cotter, who read some of my writings and also encouraged me to continue writing. I also would like to acknowledge Spero's cousin, James Kotsilibas-Davis, who read my manuscript and gave me several helpful suggestions. James is the author of several books; two about the Barrymore's, one about Myrna Loy and he co-authored a picture book about Marilyn Monroe, with Milton H. Greene.

May God rest James' soul. James passed away in 2002, at the young age of 61. So, you see, it's not my fault if you don't like my story. It's their entire fault. They kept encouraging me.

D.A.D.

About the Author

I come from a humble background. My father was Irish and my mother was German. It was an odd mixture that lasted only 13 years. Our mother raised 3 children single-handed. She worked as a secretary for 45 years for the George A. Hormel Co., now known as Hormel Foods.

My sister, brother and I went to Catholic School and had a good education. I am the baby in the family. My brother, Don, was a T.V. news Anchor and weather man. When he retired he opened a Game Store and called himself "The Game Warden"; my sister, Diana, was a model in New York City, and she married and had five children and about 9 grandchildren and 3 great grandchildren; my half sister, Lou Ann, lives in Blaine, Minnesota, and she has three children and five grandchildren.

I married, Spero K. Davis in 1957, and we have four beautiful children and 6 beautiful grandchildren.

In 1995, at the young age of 63, I had a heart attack and I died. I was revived by the Paramedics after about 12 minutes into my death and I came out of it with all my faculties. **God bless and keep Paramedics safe everywhere.**

I believe I am still here for a reason, so I started writing. I write whatever pops into my head. I started with my Memoirs and onto this Novel. I have written, so far, 18 poems that just seem to flow out of my psyche, which I never thought I could do. I then wrote a short story, "Am I Dreaming", about a friend of Spero's who was in a plane crash. I have changed everyone's name and made it fiction. I have also written two children's stories, "Little Monty Visits Grandpa's Farm" and "Little Monty Makes a New Friend". I self-published the first one, which can be found in Amazon.com—just type in Yia Yia Davis and that will take you directly to the children's book. I also wrote an Essay on my "Theory of Religion" (The Meaning of Life). I'm still working on that one.

Now I'm alone. My sweet, loving husband, Spero, is in a nursing home in Perry. He has Alzheimer's. It is so sad to see this intelligent man waist away to this state of nothingness.

I hope I'm around for many more years to get everything down on paper that my psyche needs to dispense.

Thanks for reading my Novel. DAD